Diana Carter
P.O. Box 300795
Waterford, MI 48330
248-872-3015
diana.carter44@gmail.com

I0593975

THE SISTER FACTOR: DIAMOND'S FIGHT FOR JUSTICE

By

Diana Carter

OTHER BOOKS WRITTEN BY DIANA CARTER

BROKEN PROMISES SERIES:

BROKEN PROMISES:	BROKEN PROMISES:	BROKEN PROMISES:
SHATTERERD DREAMS	WHEN SHATTERED	SHATTERRED DREAMS:
	BECOME REALITY	THE FINAL CHAPTER

DARK REVENGE: IN THE NAME OF JUSTICE:
THE TREY STORY STORY   THE ERICA BLACKSTONE
                                CHRONICLES

The Sister Factor: Diamond's Fight for Justice

Mystery/Family Drama

All Rights Reserved

Copyright © 2018 by Diana Carter

This book is a work of fiction. Names, characters, places, and incidents are the product of the author's imagination or are used fictitiously. Any resemblance to actual events, locales, or persons, living or dead, is coincidental.

This book may not be reproduced, transmitted, or stored in whole or in part by any means, including graphic, electronic, or mechanical without the express written consent of the publisher except in the case of brief quotations embodied in critical articles and reviews.

LET'S DO THIS PUBLISHING, LLC
P.O. Box 300795
Waterford, MI 48330

ISBN 13: 978-0-9997106-1-6

Cover Designed by Professional Instant Printing. All Rights Reserved

PRINTED IN THE UNITED STATES OF AMERICA

Dedication

I would like to thank God, first and foremost, for being such a positive role model in my life. He has given me the strength to move on when I wanted to give up. Without Him, life wouldn't have the same meaning. This book is a special dedication to my late sister Marcella Leona Williams. She was a great inspiration to me and to those she loved. She showed me what it means to have strength and character. As I continue to write additional books in this series, I hope to bring to my readers the enjoyment I had in writing them.

Acknowledgements

To say God knows all and sees all is an understatement. He will be there when you need Him the most and will never let you down. Writing books has fulfilled a lifelong dream, and I hope to continue to share my stories with my family, friends, and readers. This series will be similar and different from the *Broken Promises* series. *The Sister Factor* is about the lives of four sisters from a wealthy family that has issues with communication, trust, and unity. The first book is about Diamond the oldest of the four Morgan sisters. Diamond faces the challenge of finding her missing parents that were vacationing in Las Vegas.

To a special friend in my life, Athena Dumas, who has enlightened me to the fact that it is good to help others, but make sure during the process of helping them you aren't hindering their ability to do things for themselves. To Karen Walker, special thanks for being a great sounding board and an awesome person. I would also like to acknowledge my best friend Karen Whyte for all the support she has continued to give me throughout our friendship, even when it wasn't an easy thing to do. With her support, I was able to get through some of the roughest times in my life. A special thanks to another dear friend,

Carol Smith. Carol has shown me what real strength is. I will always thank God for putting her in my life. Lastly, I would like to thank Sarah Abraham with all my heart. Sarah made all of this possible by giving me the push I needed. I will always be grateful to Sarah and see her as the one person that gave me the courage to live my dream. As I continue to write this series, I hope to entertain readers with an exciting reading experience that will make the characters feel like part of their family.

God's blessings,

Diana Carter

Chapter One

Atlanta

The tension between them was so palpable it almost hummed like an electric volt. Seated at the table where they had once shared so many loving memories, Diamond stared at her sisters as if they were strangers in a restaurant. This was their first time together in their parents' home since Diamond's wedding. Busy lives and different paths kept them apart. Now that they were forced to come together, Diamond, the oldest of the Morgan sisters, decided to break the ice.

"Guys, I'm really scared. This is the first time Mom and Dad have been away without reaching out to one of us every day or two. They haven't even been in contact with our grandparents or Auntie Niecy." Di, as everyone called her, sat at the head of the table.

"Di, you need to stop being so melodramatic! You act like they've been gone forever. It's only been a week," said Krystal, the youngest.

"No, it's been more like ten days. If you cared about anybody besides yourself, you would have known how long they've been away," Diamond said.

Dior, the peacemaker of the bunch, intervened. "Come on you guys. I thought we came here to figure out what happened to Mom and Dad, not pick on one another."

"I was the last one to talk to them and that was three days ago. If we communicated with each other more, we would have known that none of us hadn't heard from them in days." Kristina added.

"There's nothing we can do about that now. We need to focus on why our parents haven't reached out to anyone," Dior said.

"Okay, let's recap. Mom and Dad left here ten days ago to go to Vegas. They let us know they arrived safely. I talked to Mom and Dad three days ago around ten o'clock in the morning, Vegas time. They were having the time of their lives. Kristie, you said you talked to them that evening, and they were about to have dinner, right?" Diamond was an attorney, questioning witnesses and discovering truth was her passion. At Kristie's slight head nod, Diamond barreled on. "So as far as we know there hasn't been any other contact since then. Is this accurate?"

"Well, I still don't see the big deal. They probably just wanted a break from everything. It couldn't have been easy raising all of us and not having a real vacation toting us along with them. Once Kristie moved out, they may have finally figured out they could do some of the things they've been dreaming of doing. I know that's how I would feel."

The other three sisters rolled their eyes at Krystal.

"Krystal, will you please just shut up if you can't offer any concern or sympathy?"

"Di, how many times do I have to tell all of you guys to stop trying to boss me around? Just because I'm the youngest doesn't mean I'm going to let you guys push me around." Krystal folded her arms, pouting.

"No one is trying to push you around, Krystal. We just want to come up with a feasible plan to see how we can start to search for Mom and Dad," Diamond explained.

"I'm sorry, guys. I'm jet-lagged and my body is still working on Paris time. I think we should check with the hotel first, since neither Mom nor Dad are answering their cell phones." Krystal suggested.

"I did call the hotel, and they said they couldn't give out any information over the phone. They transferred me to Mom and Dad's room, but the phone just kept ringing. I think one of us may have to take a trip there since we can't get any answers over the phone." Diamond gave her sisters an option.

Di, I think you should be the one to go since you're the oldest and smartest about handling situations like this. Dior and I can work things from here. I don't want to have to stay in this big house by myself." Krystal offered.

"Unfortunately, I have to agree with Krystal. Di, you are best equipped to handle this situation. Besides, I can't take off from work right now, and Kristie can't travel," Dior said.

"Have all of you forgotten, I'm a newlywed? Why should it be on me when I have a new husband and a trial to prepare for on top of that?" Diamond asked.

"Please, Di. Go see what's happened with Mom and Dad. I would go with you, but I'm just too afraid of the risk to travel," Kristina pleaded.

Diamond sighed. "I'll have to run this past Dillon, but it shouldn't be a problem for me to get away for a few days. Dior, you and Krystal will have to pick up the slack back here."

"Why do you have to always boss us around? We're not stupid." Krystal rolled her eyes at Diamond.

"All of this is getting us nowhere. I'm going home to talk to Dillon. I'll drop you off at home, Kristie. Dior can go get what she'll need from her place and stay here with the crybaby." Diamond knew her last comment would make Krystal furious, but she didn't care.

Chapter Two

Diamond was able to get a flight out for the following afternoon. She gave her husband a big hug and went to board the plane. During the flight, Diamond thought about the baby Dillon wanted so badly. Although, she didn't want to take the time off from work, she wouldn't mind having a set of boy and girl twins so she would only have to experience pregnancy and childbirth one time. She had stopped taking birth control a few months ago to surprise Dillon once she became pregnant. Diamond missed her husband already and hoped this would be a short trip.

She needed answers. Not only was she worried about her missing parents, but her newest client, Phillip Alvin Evans was kind of on the shady side. He had been charged with possession of firearm, assault and battery, and disturbing the peace. Diamond needed to figure out how to get around the gun charge with Phil's record. She hoped she could get him off without any jail time, but definitely wanted to keep his sentence as light as possible. The other charges wouldn't be as difficult to argue because he wasn't the villain. This was the first time Diamond had ever taken a domestic violence case. She wouldn't normally represent someone charged with assault and battery against a woman, but Phil was a close friend of Dillon's cousin Dante, who was more like a brother to her husband than a cousin.

Diamond loved being an attorney. She had decided at ten years old, when Krystal was, born that she would be an attorney. She figured if her parents had to have another child, the least they could have done was give her a little brother to boss around. Instead she got Krystal.

Three younger sisters were as good a place as any to hone her natural ability to persuade others to her way of thinking. Bold and brassy, Diamond never backed down from defending truth or convincing others when she was right. Diamond was tired, but she knew that same passion and defense of truth was what she needed to see her way through both of these cases. When the plane landed, she caught a cab from McCarran Airport to Caesars Palace hotel where her parents were staying.

"My name is Diamond Morgan-Washington and I am here to check on my parents' disappearance," She told the front desk clerk at the hotel.

"As I told you over the phone, Mrs. Washington, I can't give you any information about our guests. I would advise you to place a missing persons report with the police if you are that concerned."

"I don't have time for your foolishness. I want to speak to the manager," Diamond said frustrated.

The manager, Mr. Pittman was called, and within a few minutes, he approached Diamond. "How can I help you Mrs. Washington?"

"I'm here to find out information regarding my missing parents, Nick and Bethany Morgan." Diamond explained.

"I see. Why don't you check into your room and have the desk clerk to page me once you are settled?"

Diamond was situated within fifteen minutes. After meeting back up with the hotel manager, they slowly approached the two-bedroom tower penthouse registered to her parents. A DO NOT DISTRUB sign hung on the door.

"How long do you let the sign stay out before you check on your guests?" Diamond asked.

Mr. Pittman hesitated, "The room was cleaned two days ago, but your parents weren't there at the time and the cleaning staff was told to put the sign back out."

The manager knocked on the door and waited a beat before inserting the key card. The room was still clean and nothing was out of place. Diamond noticed her parents' clothes and suitcases were still in the master suite closet, and their personal items were still in the bathroom. She asked the manager if she could have some time alone in her parents' room. She thought he would say no, but he nodded his head and left the room.

Diamond sat on the bed and called her husband and her sisters to give them an update. She told them she was about to take a shower and get something to eat. She would start the search first thing in the morning. Her call to Kristina was the longest because she wanted to make sure her sister wasn't putting too much stress on herself. Kristina told her she called Junior to see if he had heard from their dad and he said, *"He wasn't the chosen one, so he would be the last one their dad would call."* Diamond was put out with herself for not contacting their older brother. She and her sister talked a few minutes more and then hung up. Diamond stepped into the hallway, closing her parents' hotel door behind her. She went to her room. After a long day, the showered beckoned. But first, she mapped out the steps she would initiate in the morning to find her parents.

Chapter Three

The next morning, Diamond was awakened by incessant knocking on her door. Startled, she shook her head trying to remember where she was. She glanced at the clock, "10:30, oh my god. "Just a second please." She grabbed the bath robe furnished by the hotel and went to answer the door.

"Good morning, Mrs. Washington. I hope we aren't disturbing you too early. I brought, Edward by to personally apologize for not being as helpful as possible when you inquired about your parents yesterday." Mr. Pittman, the hotel manager, she met with yesterday held the rude desk clerk by the sleeve of his uniform.

"I appreciate both of you taking the time to do this, but what about my parents? Is there any word on their whereabouts?"

The manager shook his head. "I'm sorry, mam. I regret to say we still don't have any additional information regarding your parents. Once you're ready, we can assist you in placing a missing persons report with our local police department."

"Fine. Just give me twenty minutes, and I'll meet you in the lobby." Diamond closed the door. She wanted to check in with Dillon before she met with the manager and the police.

Dior sat in her parents' family room with her baby sister, Krystal. The sisters were worried about Kristina's pregnancy. They didn't want anything to happen to this baby. They had a nephew Joseph Alexander Morgan (Joe). He was their older brother, Junior's son, but they didn't see him that often. Kristina walked into the room and gave both of her sisters a big hug. "Big sister," she said to Dior as she hugged her.

"How are you feeling, Kristie?" Dior asked. Since Di wasn't there to take control, she knew the task fell on her. Dior knew her parents would want to make sure Kristie continued to have a stress-free, viable and healthy pregnancy. Still, Dior couldn't stop herself from asking.

Dior continued, "What are we going to do if something bad happened to Mom and Dad?"

"We can't think like that, Dior. Let's wait and see what, Di comes up with and we can take it from there," Kristina said.

"I know you guys think I'm insensitive, but I don't see the need to push the panic button. I know it doesn't look good that Mom and Dad haven't contacted anyone the last few days, but maybe they just wanted some time alone." Krystal was still in her 'everything is alright attitude.'

"Krystal, you need to stop thinking this isn't a big deal. Mom and Dad may be in trouble, and we have to be ready to help Di if she needs us," Kristina said.

"I'm sure Di will take care of things like always, by bossing us around," Krystal said.

"Krystal, I agree with Kristie. We must get serious about this because it looks as though something bad has happened to Mom and Dad," Dior wrung her hands.

"Okay, guys, I'm terrified. Is that what you want to hear? Will you all feel better now that you know I'm afraid something has happened to Mom and Dad?" Krystal threw up her hands. "What are we going to do if they don't come back?"

"The best thing we can do is wait and see what Di comes up with. We just need to chill out and maybe call Junior over to see if he can offer some assistance." Dior knew Krystal didn't want to hear what Junior had to say, but it was his father too that was missing.

On the other side of town, Junior sat in his mom's living room sharing with her that he thought something bad had happened to his dad and step-mom. He didn't like to bring his dad and stepmom up too often because it always sent his mom into a rage, about how his dad, had the nerve to leave them for the hired help. Bethany, Junior's step-mom had been Nick's executive assistant. Junior had heard this story so many times he knew each word his mom would say before she said it.

"Junior, why are you over here wasting my time talking about the deserter and his slut? What do you want me to say? I'm sorry something bad may have happened to them. Well, I'm not, and I refused to pretend that I care about either of them."

"Come on, Ma. No one in the family has heard from them in three days. That's something to be concerned about."

"Maybe they just want to be left alone. I know if I had a daughter like that youngest girl of theirs, I would run to the ends of the earth to get away from her."

"Ma, you need to stop harping on Krystal. She was spoiled by so many people, she thinks the world revolves around her. You know it had to be hard on her to have a successful modeling career at such a young age."

"Junior, how many times do I have to tell you to stop making excuses for that little demon? Trouble follows everywhere her selfish ass happens to be."

"Ma, can we talk about something else, like your upcoming sixtieth birthday? I think we should do something special to celebrate this milestone."

"How are you going to top what y'all did for the deserter's milestone? You and those girls went all out. I'm sure mine will be on a much lower scale."

"Well, Ma, you're right about that because it will mostly be up to Jalissa and I, and we don't have the kind of money to pull something off like we did for Dad. The girls, and the rest of the family, pitched in. That's why we were able to pull off Dad's celebration."

"Now you have to make my day even worse by bringing up that good for nothing idiot you call a wife. When are you going to get someone worthy of you? You have a Masters in Community Counseling. You should be working beside the deserter." Melissa said.

"Ma, I think it's time for me to go. Let me know what you would like to do for your birthday. But remember, whatever we do, Jalissa and Joe will be involved. They are your family too." Junior was trying to show his mom respect, but she always had to say something bad about Jalissa. Junior walked out the door before his mom had the chance to say something else negative.

Chapter Four

Diamond dreaded her meeting with the manager and the police, but knew she couldn't put it off any longer. She took the elevator to the lobby, where they stood waiting for her. The hotel manager escorted the two detectives and Diamond to a small conference room directly behind the front desk. Before they took a seat, the lead detective extended his arm and introduced himself and his partner. Detective Ryan Plummer, the lead detective was taller than his partner and seemed more amiable. His partner Detective John Walters was stockier and more closed off.

"Mrs. Washington, do you have any recent pictures of your parents?" Detective Plummer asked.

Diamond handed over the picture. "We took this family picture a few months ago."

"Nice looking couple. So, you're saying none of your family or friends have heard from your parents for the last three days?"

"That's correct. My parents called my sisters or me every day since they have been on vacation up until three days ago. We checked with other family members and friends and they haven't had any contact neither."

"Okay, Mrs. Washington. We'll get started on this case right away. First, we need to collect some details from you about your parents for the missing persons report. And then, we'll start by checking local hospitals and other usual places."

"What do you mean by other usual places, Detective?" Diamond asked.

Detective Plummer looked at his partner, "Churches, tour sites, and other public places tourists like to frequent. And, hmm," The detective cleared his throat and fidgeted," Also…the morgue."

"Why are you assuming something bad happened to them?"

"I'm not assuming anything, Mrs. Washington. I'm just saying we have to explore all our options. Our job is to help you find your parents. If this is unusual behavior for your parents, then something is preventing them from making contact. We'll also run a check on their credit cards and cell phones."

"Their cell phones go straight to voicemail and there is no activity on their credit cards. My parents are responsible people, Detective Plummer. They would not go days without contacting someone in the family or their closest friends. Maybe it would be a good idea to start the investigation here at the hotel since this is where they disappeared."

"Mrs. Washington, we have already conducted an investigation here at the hotel. We care about our guests and regard their comfort and safety to the upmost," Mr. Pittman interjected.

"As you should, with the amount of money you're charging. And, if that's the case, why wasn't my family notified that my parents hadn't been in their room for the last three days?"

"As I explained to you last night, the room was cleaned a few days ago, but when our guests put their DO NOT DISTURB sign on the door, we try to give them the privacy they request."

The detectives stood. "Okay, Mrs. Washington. We need your contact information, and we'll be in touch with you as soon as we have any details to report. Detective Plummer said.

By the way, Detective Walters asked, "How long will you be in town?"

Diamond had to refrain from rolling her neck. "I'll be staying until we find my parents, Detective.

"That's helpful for us to know, Mrs. Washington. We'll know where to find you when we have something to report," Detective

Plumber handed Diamond his card and she gave him her card.. "Good day, ma'am," He offered and the detectives left the conference room.

Diamond remained seated. She was frustrated.

"Look, Mrs. Washington, we're doing everything within our power to find out what happened to your parents," Mr. Pittman assured her.

"I'll say this again, Mr. Pittman, we should have been notified when there was no activity from my parents' suite."

"Mrs. Washington, I'll have a full report of your parents' activities during their stay here for you later this evening."

"Thank you, Mr. Pittman. I appreciate your assistance," Diamond stood and left the conference room.

She returned to her room and called her husband and sisters with an update. Diamond knew she needed to start the preliminary work for Phil's case, but she wanted to rest a bit after talking to her family. She sat at the desk in her room and let her mind wander back to her childhood. At twelve, Diamond was doing so well in middle school the principal suggested to her parents that Diamond skip the seventh grade. They talked to Diamond to see how she felt about it. Diamond was eager to do it, so her parents agreed.

High school was a different environment for Diamond once she got there. She was okay being in a higher grade when she was in middle school, but high school was on a different level and she had to adjust. The kids were older and didn't seem to want to be bothered with her. The first few months were difficult until she met the girl that would become her best friend, fifteen-year-old Danielle Latreese Mitchell or Dani for short. As the co-captain of the cheerleading team, Danielle was popular with the in crowd. Although Diamond was thirteen and young to be in high school, she didn't let anyone intimidate her. She joined the student government and the debate teams, and Danielle talked her into joining the cheerleading team.

Diamond smiled as the ringtone on her cell phone began to play. She knew it was Kristie. No matter how distant or strained her relationship could be with her other siblings; she and Kristie would always be tight. Eager to hear a voice from home, she answered the phone.

"Hey, little sister, how are things going back home?"

"You would know if you had answered my calls earlier."

"Krystal. Why are you calling me from Kristie's phone?" Krystal was the last person Diamond wanted to talk to right now. "And what are you talking about? This is the first time my phone rang since I got back from the meeting."

"Sure it is. Anyway, I was calling to see if you could talk Dillon into doing a shoot with me."

"Krystal, why are you calling me with this foolishness? You know I have my hands full with the search for Mom and Dad, and my new case."

"Di, it will only take you a few minutes to call Dillon and talk him into doing this favor for me."

"Why don't you ask him yourself? Besides, I don't think he has the time to do a shoot with his caseload at the center."

"I did call him, but he rushed me off the phone before I could even explain all the details. You know he doesn't want to be bothered with me at times."

"I'll see what I can do, Krystal, but it won't be until later. I'm about to take a short nap."

"Fine, I don't know why I called you. I should have known you wouldn't take the time to help me when I'm need. It's a shame I had to call you from Kristie's phone in order to talk to you."

"Listen, Krystal, stop your damn whining. I told you I would call Dillon later. But don't be surprised if he says no because this is a busy time of the year for him at the center."

"You can get him to say yes if you wanted to. Just remember, I'm a part of this family too. Even though I'm independent, I can use help from my big sisters every once in a while." Before Diamond could say anything else, Krystal disconnected their call.

Krystal was so damn selfish. She didn't even ask if there was any news about Mom and Dad. Why is she working anyway when she always complained about Atlanta not having any pizzazz in the modeling industry? Krystal was just one more thing that had gotten under her skin this morning. The detectives. That hotel manager. As if that wasn't enough, Diamond felt utterly spent. She needed a nap.

Chapter Five

"I just can't believe your sister. Why does she find it so hard to lift one little finger to help me? Isn't that what older siblings are supposed to do for younger siblings?" Krystal flopped down on the sofa next to Dior. She was so upset with Diamond she thought her head would explode.

"Krystal, it may have something do with all that's going on right now. We need to focus on finding Mom and Dad. That's where Di's head is right now, and that's where it should be, not scheduling photo shoots," Kristina said.

"I have to agree with Kristie on this one, Krystal. Di has a lot on her plate, and since none of us were able to fly to Vegas with her, we shouldn't be bothering her with something that could wait until she gets back home," Dior added.

"I get all of that, but I need to work to get my mind off how worried I am about Mom and Dad. My agent has been trying to get Dillon to do a photo shoot for about a year now, but Dillon always claims he's too busy at the center. I know he could get someone else to do something around that place," Krystal said.

"Krystal, I think all of us is guilty of letting you get your way too much, and now you think everything should revolve around you. Give us a break. You're going to have to learn there's more to life than expecting people to move to the beat of your drum," Kristina said.

"Oh my God, you sound just like a Di clone right now, Kristie. I know the world doesn't revolve around me, but my agent is counting on me to set this shoot up with Dillon. When I talked to Dillon earlier, he just brushed me off. That's the only reason I asked for Di's help." Krystal paused. "Wait a minute. You can talk to Dillon for me, Kristie. He'll listen to you."

"Krystal, I'm not going to ask that man to do something he's no longer interested in doing."

"I forgot. You don't care about anything in life, but your husband and having babies." Krystal's face turned red. She knew she had overstepped, but before she could apologize, Kristina excused herself and went upstairs.

"Krystal, how could you be so insensitive? You need to apologize to Kristie and watch what you say," Dior said.

Tears rolled down Krystal's face, "I didn't mean to upset Kristie. I was just trying to get my point across that since she doesn't have or want a career, it's hard for her to understand the dynamics of the business world."

"Nevertheless, you should never be so hurtful, especially to your sister. She's been nothing but supportive of you."

"I'll apologize as soon as she comes back down. I really didn't mean to hurt her feelings. It's just... sometimes, I look at her and all I think about is Di getting ready to criticize me."

"Well, she isn't, Di, and you shouldn't treat Di like that neither because she would help you out if she could."

"Come on, Dior. You know all Di has to do is call Dillon and say a few sweet words to him. He would do anything she wants."

"You're still missing the point. This is not the right time. But it is time for you to go upstairs and apologize to Kristie. And, then we can start dinner.

As the girls set the dinner table, there was a knock at the door. Dior excused herself and went to answer it.

"Junior, what a nice surprise! Why didn't you use your key? Come on in. We were just about to have dinner."

"Dad and I had a few unpleasant words before his trip, and I returned my key to him in the heat of the moment."

Dior shook her head, "When are you guys going to get along? The problem is you two are too much alike." Dior and Junior reached the dining room.

"Hey, Junior, you're just in time. Let me set another plate," Kristina said.

"Thanks, Kristie…Krystal." Junior acknowledged his youngest sister, who did not return the acknowledgment.

Dior blessed the food.

"Guys, I'm really starting to get worried. I haven't spoken to Dad since the day before they left for vacation, and I don't like the way we left things." Junior said, as they dug into their meal.

"Dad wouldn't be so hard on you if you came to your senses and worked with him and Di. With your education that Dad paid a fortune for, you shouldn't be going around from one dead end temporary service agency to another, like you don't have any other options. Even if you don't want to work with Dad and Di, with a Masters from Clark Atlanta University, you have options of obtaining plenty of high paying jobs," Krystal scolded.

"Krystal, why do you bring this up almost every time you see me? Being stuck in a stuffy office all day isn't for me. I tried to make Dad understand that before he made me further my education."

"You could've tried harder. Pressure was put on Di to follow in Dad's footsteps after you screwed up so badly." Krystal wouldn't let up.

"Di wanted to follow Dad, I didn't. How would you feel if you weren't allowed to pursue your dreams? You were able to start your career because the rest of us paved the way," Junior replied.

"Listen, guys, we should be brainstorming about how we're going to help Di with the search, not at each other throat," Kristina pleaded.

"I agree with Kristie. I think we could start by calling family and friends and put a timeline together so we can figure out the last person that spoke with Mom and Dad," Dior suggested.

"That's a great idea, Dior. I can make a call list and divide it between the four of us," Kristina offered.

"Make that three, Kristie. I don't feel like talking to people that doesn't like me," Krystal said.

"Krystal, cut this foolishness out right now." Dior pounded on the table, accentuating each word," "You will help with the calling or anything else that needs to be done. It's time for you to grow the hell up and think about others. This isn't about you. It's about Mom and Dad. They could be dead for all we know."

Krystal was speechless. Silent tears fell from her eyes when, she finally spoke. "Kristie, you can divide that list into four." The siblings talked for a few minutes longer before saying their goodbyes.

Chapter Six

Dillon was just about to lock the doors to the youth center when Dante and Phillip came barging in. "What you hoodlums doing on this side of town?" Dillon said with a big smile on his face.

"Man, I'm going crazy. When is your wife coming back so she can take care of this bullshit Whitney got me caught up in?" Phillip asked.

"You need to chill, man. You don't know how hard it was to convince Di to take your case. You know she can't stand physical violence towards women."

"What about physical violence towards men? That chick is crazy as hell. All I wanted to do was visit my son, and she had the nerve to have a trick over there. I told her I wasn't going to abide by that shit," Phillip frowned.

"And, look where your temper has gotten you. Di will have to work like mad to get the gun charge dropped. As for the other charges, they won't be easy with your record, but I know she can work something out."

"I know that shit was stupid about the gun, but I just had a feeling before I went over there that something wasn't right."

35

"If you had that feeling, why the hell you take your knuckle head butt over there?" Dante asked.

"Man, you stupid? I know you just heard me tell DW that crazy ass chick had that fool around my son. I've been trying to get my parents to file for custody since they know the living arrangements little man has to deal with." Phillip was the only one that called Dillon by his initials.

"Why don't you get yourself together and take care of your son, man? I see it all too often where younger parents slack off and expect their parents to be responsible for raising a child they didn't create," Dillon said.

"Man, you make it sound like I'm a dead-beat dad, but that's so far from the truth. I've been taking care of my son since the day he was born, but Whitney is giving me a hard time because I don't want her sorry ass anymore."

"That may be true, but the courts will judge you by your legal actions. And the way your situation is at the moment, you'll be lucky to get visitation," Dillon said.

"That's one of the reasons I want my parents to have custody. Then I'll know little man will be taken care of if I have to go to prison. Plus, I'll get a chance to see him. Besides, Whitney has her hands full with her other four rug-rats."

"Phil, we tried to warn you about that chick before you hooked up with her, but you wouldn't listen to us," Dante shook his head.

"You guys know that crazy girl hounded me."

"What you expect? Four kids and no daddies around, you were a good catch," Dillon said.

"You were a lost cause, bruh. That woman had you whipped," Dante added.

Dillon noticed the beaten look on Phillip's face and knew he needed to rescue Phillip from Dante's teasing.

"What y'all come over for anyway? "Get out," he chuckled. "It's time for me to close up shop anyway. Meet me at my house in an hour." Dillon rushed the guys out and finished locking down the building.

Diamond's short nap turned into a few glorious hours of sleep, but at least she felt rested.

She hoped that spooky manager had her information ready. His report better be detailed, or she was going to be all over him. She was both anxious and afraid of what the report might contain. She didn't have the feeling something bad happened to her parents, but their lack of contact was so unlike them. She knew she had to be prepared to face whatever information came her way. The phone rang just as she finished freshening up.

"Diamond Morgan-Washington," she answered.

"Mrs. Washington, this is Mr. Pittman from the hotel. I was calling to inform you the report will be delivered to your room by seven o'clock this evening."

"Thank you, Mr. Pittman. I look forward to receiving it. Any word from the police yet?"

"Not to my knowledge, and it's my understanding that unless it has something to do specifically with the hotel, the police will contact you directly with their findings."

"What do you mean if it has something to do specifically with the hotel? Of course, it would have something to do with the hotel. This is where my parents disappeared."

"I understand your concern, Mrs. Washington. However, the details in the report suggest there might be other factors to consider.

"I'll make that determination after I've read the report. And please ensure your contact information is listed on the report in case I have questions," Diamond said.

"Mrs. Washington, I'm not your enemy. If you need to reach me regarding the details of the report or any concerns about your stay at Caesars Palace, just call the front desk."

"I'll be the judge of that, Mr. Pittman. After, I read the report." Diamond hung up the phone.

Chapter Seven

Atlanta

Junior and his sisters called everyone on the list Kristie had divided between the four of them. Now the family room of his dad and stepmom's home was filled with family and friends. *Di can have this oldest sibling is in charge stuff. This is for the birds,* Junior thought to himself. He dreaded having to tell his family Dad and Mama Beth were missing and tried to hold off long as possible. He didn't want to upset his grandparents and auntie, but he couldn't delay the inevitable.

Junior clapped his hands to get everyone's attention. "Uh, we'd like to thank everyone for coming over. I'm sure y'all are wondering why we asked you all to meet us here at Dad and Mama Beth's." He looked down at the floor. "Dad and Mama Beth are missing. It's been more than three days since they've made contact with any of us, and we're concerned."

Questions and gasps of shock erupted around the room. Dior went over in front of her dad's parents, Justin and Eunice Morgan. "Di went to Vegas to investigate," Junior continued. "What we plan to do on our end is to create a timeline of the last time everyone in this room talked to Dad and Mama Beth."

"I don't understand. There's no way Beth wouldn't get in touch with one of us." Bethany's mom became hysterical. "Oh my God, what happened to my baby?" Kristina tried to console her sobbing grandmother. Nick's mom began to cry. Nick's dad decided it was too much for the mothers to bear and excused the three of them from the family meeting. Dior suggested Kristina go with them so she could rest for a little while.

After the grandparents and Kristina left, Dior explained the situation to her auntie and her parents' best friends. "We're sorry we didn't tell you guys sooner. We thought once Di arrived in Vegas she would have good news to report, and this situation would be resolved quickly." She rubbed her hands across her face.

"What do we do next?" Nick's sister Denise asked.

"We pray Di will have some good news for us soon. She is supposed to get a detailed report from the manager this evening of Mom and Dad's activities since they checked into the hotel," Dior said.

"And, since most of Dad and Mama Beth's family and friends are here, we should get started on creating a timeline. As matter of fact, let me go grab my laptop." Junior said.

When he returned, he created a chart in Excel with the date, day, time, and the names of everyone in attendance, along with a few others from the list of calls they made earlier. They spent the next half hour creating the chart.

It was determined that Vince, his dad's best friend was the last to talk to Nick and Denise was the last to talk to Bethany.

"Well, I think we've done all we can do here," Junior said. "The girls and I really appreciate your input. I'll get this information to Di as soon as possible. I'm sure it will help her tremendously. In the meantime, why don't everyone go home and get some rest. We don't know how long it will be before we have news.

The grandparents were still distraught, Denise took her parents' home, and Dior took Bethany's mom Stacey home. The others planned on staying to see what they could do to help out with the search. Reggie, Kristina's husband, had already picked up Kristina. Junior promised to keep everyone posted and told them it was best they went to get some rest because they didn't know how long it would be before they had any news to report. Once Dior made it back, she, Junior, and Krystal met in the family room to recap.

"It's good to know Dad and Mama Beth were doing well a few days ago," Junior said.

"Junior, do you think, Mom and Dad are still alive?" Krystal asked.

"Yes, I do, but I'm scared something bad has happened to keep them from making contact," Junior answered.

"I feel the same as Junior. I don't feel they are hurt or anything like that," Dior agreed.

"I have to go and lay down for a little while. My head is spinning with all the people that invaded our home today." Krystal went to her room.

"Well, sis, I better head home. Jalissa has to run a few errands, and I promised to stay with Joe," Junior gathered his belongings and headed home.

Dillon arrived home twenty minutes before Dante and Phillip arrival. They decided to meet downstairs in Dillon's man cave.

They were chilling around the pool table when Philip broke down. "I'm in some real deep shit."

"Not trying to beat you while you're down man, but I know you're not just realizing you're in big trouble?" Dante asked.

"I don't want to go to prison. I hate the way I let that stupid ass woman get next to me." Phillip was frustrated.

"What's done is done man. We just want you to know we're in your corner and we'll be there to support you, Dillon said.

"I know, Di will do all she can for me, but I need her to talk to my parents to convince them to get Lil man out of that hell house." Phillip looked at Dillon with pleading eyes.

"Phil, you will have to do that on your own. Di has too much on her plate as is dealing with her missing parents and spoiled ass baby sister. Plus, she's been worrying about her lazy ass brother too," Dillon said.

"I'm sorry, man. You're right. It just came down on me. My son is the most important person in my life. Outside of me and my family, Lil man doesn't have any positive role models in his life. I know Whitney will try to keep him away from my family if I go to prison."

"Just stay away from her, man. When Di gets back, she will work on getting you visitation with your son if the worst happens," Dillon said.

"Okay, Dante let's roll. I got to try to get some sleep. This shit has been keeping me up at night."

"I will hit you guys up in a day or two with an update on Di's parents and the case." Dillon walked Dante and Phillip to Dante's car and wondered if his wife would be able to keep Phillip from going to prison.

Chapter Eight

The manager greeted Diamond with a grim look on his face. He handed her the folder and told her the report started with her parents' arrival and ended with the day she arrived to begin her search for them. Diamond, took the report, thanked Mr. Pittman and closed the door. She went over to the desk and said a prayer before looking at what was inside.

Nick and Bethany checked into Caesars Palace on Friday, January 11th, at five-thirty pm. They had a late dinner in the lounge and returned to their room. According to the report, the next day they were up early. They asked about tours and special events for the weekend. After gathering information, they went with other tourists on a two-hour art exhibit tour. Diamond smiled. She knew her mom had dragged her dad to that event.

She decided to wait and deal with the report the next day with fresher eyes. She was disappointed she hadn't heard from the detectives. Junior had emailed her the timeline chart the family put together, so she decided to print it out and add it to the report the manager had given her. Diamond missed Dillon. Talking to him over the phone wasn't enough for her. She missed her sisters too, even Krystal which was a surprise. But, Junior seemed to be handling things well back home with the girls' help.

Diamond was shocked to hear that Krystal mostly behaved herself at the family meeting and was actually helping out after Dior laid into her. Krystal hadn't asked Diamond to talk to Dillon again about the photo shoot, but Diamond felt a little guilty, so she called Dillon before turning in for the night to see if he would be willing to do the shoot.

"Come on, Di, why are you trying to stick me with your irritating sister?"

"Baby, it's just one shoot. Maybe she will change her attitude. It's time for the family to take some responsibility for Krystal's bad behavior. We should have been harder on her when she was younger."

"But, I wasn't around when Krystal was younger."

"Dillon, be serious."

Dillon laughed. "Okay, I'll consider it. I do want to be fair, and I know you wouldn't have touched Phil's case with a ten-foot pole if I hadn't pressured you."

"Baby, don't do it because of that. I don't want you to feel like you owe me. Speaking of Phillip, I had a chance to review his case. They are trying to railroad him."

"Hmmm, why am I not surprised?"

"So, will you do the honors of calling, Krystal, or shall I?"

"Wait a minute, Di. I said I would consider it, not that I would do it. You know how busy the center is this time of the year, and there's only so much delegating I can do."

"Alright, Dillon, sleep on it and give me your decision tomorrow. I know it would make life easier for Dior, Kristie, and Junior if Krystal had something else to do besides working on their nerves."

"Sweet dreams, Di. I love you, baby. Please take care of yourself."

"You don't have to worry about me, remember. I'm Super Woman."

"Goodnight, Super Woman. Love you, baby."

"Love you more. I'll talk to you in the morning."

Diamond hung up the phone with Dillon, but she was too restless to go to sleep. She didn't want to look at the case or the report, so she decided to take a few minutes to relax her mind by going back to her junior year in high school.

This was Diamond's first year in high school without Danielle. She would have her work cut out for her when Dior started next year. Since Dior was her sister, she wanted to pave the way as much as possible, so Dior wouldn't have some of the same challenges she had when she first started. Now that she was a junior and cheerleader captain, Diamond had responsibilities that pushed her to the limits. She knew if her grades dropped her parents would make her give up some of her activities. Since she couldn't imagine giving up anything, she pushed herself more than her parents did.

Things started to change for Diamond towards the end of her sophomore year. She began to show interest in boys, and even though she hadn't met anyone she liked, the interest was there. A few months into her junior year, she met Jason Albert Jones, and she understood what Danielle meant by finding the right one. JJ, as everyone called him was new to Ben Franklin High School. He was the most handsome boy Diamond had ever seen.

Diamond and JJ became fast friends and started dating soon after meeting each other. JJ was important to Diamond, but she never lost focus of her dreams and other responsibilities. As their relationship moved forward this became a problem, because JJ wanted to spend more time with Diamond. Time was something Diamond had little of, so their relationship began to fizzle. By the time they reached their senior year in high school, their relationship grew further apart. Diamond realized another reason they were having problems was because she wasn't ready to have sex with JJ. Towards the end of their relationship, she finally gave in but after that it seemed as if JJ lost interest in her.

Diamond wasn't happy with herself after having sex with JJ. She realized she had done it for him, not because she wanted to. She understood what Danielle was going through with DeShawn. Diamond really liked JJ, but she knew he didn't feel the same about her. She considered having sex with JJ a major mistake. A few months into their senior year, they decided to move on. Then out of the blue JJ asked her to the Homecoming dance. He reminded her they were a shoe in for king and queen since he was the captain of the football team and she was captain of the cheerleading team. Again, against her better judgment, she went to the dance with JJ. They were voted king and queen, and that night she ended up having sex with JJ again. Since she was still in love with JJ, it was hard for her to say no. Diamond chalked this up to another bad mistake and decided to focus on other important things in her life, even though her heart was broken.

She didn't tell anyone about her sexual relationship with JJ. She thought about telling Danielle or Dior, but wasn't ready for them to know how foolish she was for getting involved with someone that didn't care about her. About a month after the dance, Diamond told her mom about JJ. Bethany was understanding, but wanted Diamond to know the consequences of making such grown up decisions at her age. Diamond begged her mom not to tell her dad, because she didn't want him to be disappointed in her like he was in Junior.

The remainder of her senior year, Diamond focused on getting good grades and keeping up with her activities. She dated off and on, but not seriously. During her senior year Diamond interned at her dad's law firm. This was great for her and sealed her decision to become an attorney. Everyone in the family was so proud of her when she graduated top of the senior class and was selected valedictorian. Excited about going to Spelman in the fall, she interned with her dad through the summer and relaxed with her family. Her first year at Spelman, she commuted, but she had a goal to finish her undergrad in three years instead of the standard four and she moved on campus when she started her sophomore year.

Although, Diamond missed her family, especially Kristina, she quickly adjusted to college life. Attending an all-girls school wasn't her first choice, but the curriculum at Spelman fitted in with her goals. Coming back to the present, Diamond decided it was time for her to call it a night.

Chapter Nine

Junior pulled into his mom's driveway and debated about going in to see her. It was less than four weeks before her birthday, and she still refused to tell him what she wanted to do. A few more people on his mother's side of the family agreed to pitch in, but most of them had cut ties with her years ago when she became so hateful after his dad left them. Her celebration still wouldn't be on the level of what they did for his dad, but with the extra funds, they could pull off something nice. He got out of the car and knocked on the door, even though he had a key. Junior never used his key when his mom was home.

"Boy, how many times do I have to tell you to use your damn key? Do you get a thrill out of making me get up and walk all the way out here to let you in when all you have to do is use your key?" His mom, Melissa stomped back into her den.

"Hi, Ma, how are you doing today?" Junior ignored his mom's harsh words.

"I was fine until I had to get up and let you in when all you had to do was use your key. Use the damn thing or give it back to me."

"Ma, I'm just trying to be respectful." Junior followed his mom to the den.

"What brings you out this late to see your old helpless mom?"

"Ma, eight o'clock isn't late. And, I just wanted to see what you decided to do for your birthday." Junior knew this was a touchy subject, but he wanted to start planning.

"Boy, why you keep hounding me about my birthday? Do you think I want to think about getting older?"

"Ma, we're all getting older. We just want to do something special for you on your birthday."

"When you say we, I guess you're including that wife of yours?" Melissa gave him a side eye.

"Of course, Ma. She's part of this family. When are you going to start treating her like family? It's been fourteen years."

"That's another thing I don't need you to remind me about. It's not easy to forget the day your only child threw his life away."

"Ma, I've been thinking about a lot of things in my life lately. I think I'm ready to move my career in another direction."

"Baby, that's great news. What kind of move were you thinking about making?"

"I'm not sure. I want to talk to Jalissa first, but since I've been helping with the search for Dad and Beth (Junior had to be careful not to call her Mama Beth in front of his mom), I could do something in the line of investigative work. I feel confident in my skills to gather information."

"Damn, you were on a roll until you brought up those creatures. Why do you have to give me great news then turn around and cancel it out with horrible news?"

"Ma, please get some help. This bitterness you're carrying around can't be good for your health."

"Boy, do I look sick to you? I don't need your young ass telling me what to do with my life. I suggest you go home and try to tame that wild ass wife and son of yours."

"Ma, please. I just wanted to share my good news with you. How long have you been trying to get me to do something productive with my life?"

"Okay, Junior, let me know if there's anything I can do to assist you. I'm proud of you, baby, even if this realization had to come from your looking for the deserter and his slut."

"It's getting late, Ma. Please let me know soon what you want to do for your birthday. You're a special lady. I just want you to be treated extra special on your big day."

"I'll let you know in a day or two. Is that soon enough? And, I was just pulling your leg the other day. I don't need anything big. Your love and support is good enough for me, baby."

"I'm going to say this to Jalissa too, Ma. Please stop being so mean to each other. You two are the most important women in my life. It would be a blessing if the two of you tried to get along. Joe needs his grandma in his life."

"Okay, baby, I'll try harder for your sake. But tell that foolish girl to learn some manners."

"Ma, both of you will need to make some changes if this is going to work," Junior said before leaving.

Dillon wished for once since meeting, Diamond Lynette Morgan he could tell her no.

"Good evening, Krystal. It's Dillon. How are you doing tonight?" Dillon really didn't care how she was doing, but he was trying to be polite.

"That all depends on why you're calling me so late."

"I know you don't have the nerve to call eight-thirty late, when you think nothing of calling here all times of the night."

"My sister is available to receive calls from me anytime of the day or night since I'm in different parts of the world most of the time."

"Little girl, you about to make me break a promise to my wife with all of this crazy talk."

"What promise?"

Dillon rolled his eyes at Krystal's sickly-sweet tone.

"Look, let that agent know I'll agree to one shoot. It has to be shot in a day, and I want my share of the proceeds to be made out to the youth center."

"Yes!" Krystal squealed into the phone. "Thanks, Dillon. I'll call you as soon as I make arrangements with my agent."

"I mean it, Krystal. This is a one-time shoot, so don't get any ideas in your head that I'll be doing this again anytime in the future. I'm still a newlywed, and I have too much to do at the center."

"Okay already, I get the point. Thank you, brother-in-law, I love you."

This fool is so phony, Dillon thought to himself. Just a few days ago she wanted to have him horse-whipped for not agreeing to the shoot, now she was all into him.

"Do you have any idea how much your sister loves you?"

"Dillon, you won't regret this. I'll be in touch with you sometime tomorrow."

It wasn't lost on Dillon that Krystal ignored his question. "You do that. I want to get this over with."

"Okay, okay I told you I get the point."

"I've got to get some rest so make sure you make this happen real soon. Once Di gets back home, all bets are off."

"I'll call my agent first thing in the morning to schedule the shoot and get the details to you. I hope you answer your phone and not avoid me like Di does sometimes."

Before Dillon could respond, Krystal ended the call.

Dillon wanted to strangle that ungrateful girl. *Good grief. What did I do to deserve being stuck working with Krystal again?* It had been years since they worked together, but she was more trouble than any other model he ever worked with. Dillon didn't want to waste any more energy thinking about the shoot. He jumped in the shower and waited for Diamond to call.

Chapter Ten

Diamond awoke refreshed after a good night's sleep ready to get her day started. She had a long talk with Dillon after he talked to Krystal last night. She couldn't believe it took her almost a half hour to calm him down. He kept telling Diamond, he didn't know how he was going to get through an entire shoot with Krystal when a ten-minute phone call had him ready to break her selfish ass neck. Diamond stressed how the proceeds would help with his plans for the youth center.

Diamond had met Dillon when, he was in his glory days of modeling. She remembered how Dillon loved being in front of the cameras, but now he didn't care if he ever did another shoot in his life. Diamond thought Dillon would be into women like Krystal, who was gorgeous, but that wasn't the case. Dillon chased Diamond for about six months before she realized he was serious about being with her. Dillon had told her that was new for him because he never had to chase a woman before. Both Diamond and Dillon learnt lessons about life at the beginning of their relationship.

When Krystal entered her first year in high school, she received a modeling assignment at the same agency where Dillon worked. The agency paired Krystal and Dillon to work together. Dillon confessed to Diamond that he hated working with her little sister, but didn't want anything to come between them. Diamond told Dillon she didn't know how he could put up with her for as long as he had. Not long after their talk, Dillon lost interest modeling and wanted to focus more on the youth center he had started a year before.

Diamond hoped she'd done the right thing asking Dillon to work with Krystal again. She knew how bratty her little sister could be. Diamond stood and stretched. She decided to go to the hotel's restaurant to have breakfast instead of ordering room service. And, she was glad she did because she ran into the spooky manager who always seemed to be on duty. He mentioned they had an excellent business center where she could work in peace with access to a computer, printer, scanner, and other research tools she might need in her search. Once she finished her breakfast, she went back up to her room to get her tablet and the file the manager had given her.

Diamond was impressed with the business center. The environment was state of the art, and she felt at peace and motivated to work. She spread her work out and put on a set of headphones that were attached to the computer. She started reading about the second day of her parents' trip. After they returned from their tour, they had dinner in their room, and her dad spent about an hour on the blackjack table while her mom played slots. After that, they caught a show and returned to their room about three hours later.

Diamond was about to review the information from Junior when she saw the detectives enter the business center. Diamond didn't know how she felt about their visit, but it had to mean they had something to report. She stood to meet them.

"Mrs. Washington, we were told we could find you in here," Detective Plummer said.

"I take it you have some new information about my parents."

"Yes, we do. But if you don't mind, I'd like to speak in the conference room where we can talk without being interrupted."

Diamond gathered her belongings and followed the detectives to the conference room.

Once they reached the conference room and were seated, Detective Plummer began, "Mrs. Washington, we haven't found out what happened to your parents yet, but it seems as though they aren't the only couples missing from this hotel and two others in the area."

"Oh my God! What is going on around here, Detective Plummer?"

"Of course you realize we can't disclose the full details, but there have been reports of other couples missing during the same time-frame as your parents."

"I'm confused. How can this be possible without someone knowing what's going on?" Diamond asked.

"We're still working on this, and now, with the additional information we have uncovered, this gives us more leads to follow."

"Why is it taking so long to get to the bottom of this? How many other couples are missing?"

Detective Walters said, "You have to understand, Mrs. Washington. The guests in these hotels pay for their privacy, and that's what they get. We can't tell you about the other couples. We can only discuss your parents' situation."

"Don't tell me what you can or can't discuss with me. I know the law, and I want more answers than what I'm getting from the two of you."

"We're well aware of who you are, Mrs. Washington. Your dad's reputation is infamous. With that being said, we have to take this investigation in another direction. We've covered the normal areas. Now it's time to look deeper into what, if anything connects all these missing couples."

"You need to tell me what the hell is going on around here. I know you guys have more information than what you are telling me, and I WILL NOT be put off. My parents have been missing for almost a week, and you are trying to tell me you have absolutely no idea what happened to them or the other missing couples. I'm not buying this load of bullshit." Diamond smacked the table.

"Mrs. Washington, we're telling you all that we can at the moment. Additional detectives have been assigned to this case, so you can rest assured we will have more information to report soon," Detective Plummer said.

"You guys just made this case more confusing. I expected answers and now there are more questions than answers."

"We'll keep you posted, Mrs. Washington. Please, have a nice day." The detectives stood and left the room. Diamond was boiling and must have stood too quickly because she became dizzy. She took a few deep breaths to steady herself and then made her way back to her room. She called Dillon and her sisters to let them know her stay would likely be longer than expected.

Chapter Eleven

Diamond was upset. She wanted to call her sisters first, but needed to hear Dillon's voice. He answered on the first ring.

"Hi, baby. How are you doing this morning?"

"I could be better. I just had a meeting with the detectives assigned to my parents' case, and there seems to be a more widespread problem than first anticipated."

"What did they tell you?"

Diamond relayed her conversation with the detectives.

"I don't like the way things are going. I'm headed back to the center. When I get there, I'll be delegating so I can get the next flight out."

"No, honey, you can't do that. Now isn't a good time for you to be away from the center. I'll be okay"

"This is a battle you're not going to win, Di."

"Honey, what about your promise to do the shoot with Krystal?"

"That shit can wait. This is more important. You know I could care less about the shoot or Krystal.

"Honey, you need to calm down. I still have the report to go through and the information from Junior. If you wait a couple of days before you come up, it would give you a chance to wrap things up at the center and still do the shoot with Krystal."

"No, this happening is just a sign not to do the shoot."

"Honey, please. You promised you would help her out. She's going stir-crazy in that house by herself while Dior is at work."

"Then her rude ass should do something productive, like help, Junior and the girls with the search."

"Dior said she's seeing some change in Krystal's behavior. You know change doesn't happen overnight," Diamond persisted.

"Listen, baby, find out what's going on, and I'll keep my promise. But no matter what's going on at the center or with Krystal, I'll be there with you within the next three days."

"Okay, honey, that's fair. I can't wait to see you. I miss you so much."

"I miss you too, baby. I love you. Give me a call later tonight. And be sure to keep me posted on any new details in the case."

After Dillon said goodbye, Diamond figured there was no need to avoid the inevitable and called Krystal. Explaining to Krystal that Dillon was coming to Vegas within three days didn't go well.

"What about the shoot?" Krystal whined. "I may not be able to set it up that soon."

"Then you're out of luck because it took me a while to get Dillon not to cancel altogether."

"I should've known I couldn't depend on either of you. I've already told my agent it was a go. If I cancel, it could ruin my career."

"Listen, little girl, right now your career is the last damn thing on my mind. I'm worried sick about Mom and Dad."

"I'm worried too. That's why I need to focus on work. How many times am I going to have to tell all of you I NEED TO WORK?"

"Let me talk to Kristie." Diamond had said all she was going to say to Krystal. She talked to Kristina and Junior for a few minutes then told them she had to get back to work.

"Damn, my life sucks. I may have lost my mom and dad, and now my career is down the tubes," Krystal complained.

"Krystal, have you taken a minute to think about what others may be going through? I thought Dior's setting you straight the other day would open your eyes and heart, but it seems as though her words went in one ear and out the other," Junior said.

"I don't need to hear shit from your unmotivated ass. I have a career that's important to me. It's not my fault you don't have any aspirations in your life besides upsetting and disappointing Dad."

"You guys cut it out right now. We can't keep going over the same bull every time we get together. Let's focus on Mom and Dad please. If we can't do that from now on, I won't be coming over here because I am sick of all this bickering," Kristina said.

"Kristie, calm down. You know you shouldn't be getting this upset. I would never forgive myself if something happened to you or the baby. Krystal, let's call a truce and concentrate on Dad and

Mama Beth. I was thinking of going at this from another angle, would you like to help?" Junior said.

Krystal nodded. "Let me go call my agent and set up the shoot with Dillon. Once that's out of the way, I'll give this case my full attention. I already told my agent I needed to take an indefinite break after this shoot."

"I'm proud of you, baby girl. I knew you would come around," Kristina said.

"I know I can be difficult at times, but I don't know what we're going to do if we lose Mom and Dad." Krystal said.

Junior walked across the room and gave his baby sister a big hug.

"Wow, are my eyes deceiving me?" Dior walked in and sat next to Kristina. She gave her sister a side hug and stared at Junior and Krystal.

"Don't act brand new, Dior. I told you I'll do my part. You guys just have to be more patient with me," Krystal said with tears in her eyes.

"Okay, with that being said, we have to get back to work so we can do more on this end to help Di." Junior released Krystal from their embrace.

"Good, I was able to get next week off from work, so I'll have more time to help out. Kristie, we don't want to leave you out, but with all the stress going on around here, maybe we should keep you updated over the phone," Dior suggested.

"I can do that, but I hope you guys will assign something for me to do. Reggie will be ecstatic that I'll be staying home. He's been on my back to take it easy."

"Let me work on some things and touch base with Di. I'm sure we can come up with something for you to do that won't put too much stress on you, Kristie," Junior said.

"That's a good idea, Junior, and maybe you can take Kristie home, so she won't have to wait on Reggie," Dior said.

Kristina gathered her things. After Junior and Kristina left, Krystal and Dior chatted about her phone call with Dillon.

"Why are you looking at me like that, Dior?" Krystal asked.

"Don't play dumb with me, girl. How could you think about work with all this family drama going on?"

"Why are you doing this to me, Dior? When you're at work, I'm in this big ole house doing nothing. I need to do something to keep my mind from having bad thoughts about Mom and Dad."

"You could work with Junior to occupy your time."

"You know me and that fool don't get along."

"Krystal, I think this should be a wakeup call for you to get your act together. We have let you be so dependent on us that you expect no matter what the situation, everyone to cater to your wants and needs. I'm here to tell you now, that attitude isn't going to work any longer. You're going to have to step up just like the rest of us. What I walked in on between you and Junior was touching. That's a good start."

"Dior, why are you starting to act like Di?" Krystal pouted.

"I'm not acting like Di, baby girl. I'm trying to get you to understand that all of us have to do our part to help find Mom and Dad. We don't need the usual drama you bring when you don't get your way."

"I'm trying to change, Dior. It's not going to happen overnight. I took to heart what you yelled at me during our first meeting with

Junior and Kristie. Couldn't you tell by the way I didn't let the family have it at the meeting with our grandparents?"

"I'll admit, I see a little change in your behavior, but asking Dillon to do a shoot when he has a full caseload at the center and missing Di wasn't cool."

"Dior, I thought you would understand. This is such a big boost to my career. Agents have tried to book Dillon for close to a year without any success."

"That's the point, Krystal. He doesn't want to be in that line of work any longer. Since we're not going to agree on this subject, let's talk about something else."

"I'm worried about Kristie. I don't know how we're going to be able to keep her from stressing out about Mom and Dad," Krystal said.

"I think Reggie will be able to make her take it easy. Look at you concerned about someone else. I knew you had it inside of you, baby girl."

"Dior, I love all of you guys. I just don't like the way Di bosses us around and how the rest of the family only tolerates me."

"You have to take some responsibility for that, Krystal, because sometimes you're so out of control. I know it's hard for you because you became successful at a young age, but you look down on others most of the time."

"Well, no one wants to give me credit for trying to change, but you and Kristie."

"Try harder is all I'm saying, Krystal."

"Okay, I will…after my beauty nap."

Dior shook her head. Dealing with her baby sister was like taking a step forward and then two steps back.

Chapter Twelve

Diamond gathered her materials and returned to the business center, which had a few guests in it. She sat at the workstation she had occupied earlier and opened the report she received from the hotel manager. Diamond began where she left off this morning. She paused, her review of Day 3 to jot down some notes from her meeting with the detectives. Something felt weird and sinister, but Diamond couldn't exactly put her finger on what. She decided a call to the firm's investigative team was in order. She knew there was more going on than the detectives were saying, and Mr. Pittman was disturbing. She hadn't gotten a good vibe from him since the day they met. It was definitely time to bring in her back up team to assist in this search.

When Dillon arrived, she would go around to the other hotels in the area and do more hands-on investigation. It bothered Diamond that the investigation was going so slow, and she was sure Mr. Pittman was hiding something. With a game plan mapped out, she turned her attention back to day three of her parents' stay. It seemed as though her parents wanted to take it easy on day three of their trip. They had placed the DO NOT DISTURB sign on their door and ordered room service for breakfast and lunch. Diamond thought two nights out in a row must have been a lot for her parents since their pace has slowed down over the last few years. They didn't entertain or go out as much as they used to when they were trying to build her dad's clientele in the early years.

That night, they had dinner in the hotel's lounge and caught another show before turning in. Next, Diamond looked the chart Junior sent her. He had done an excellent job. Everything was color coded to match the names, dates, and times. She knew from their conversation that Junior was on a mission not only to find their missing parents, but also to change his professional life. It seemed like he had found his calling with investigative work. He mentioned talking to their dad about joining the firm in that capacity once they were located.

Diamond had left for Vegas in such a hurry, she didn't even think to check for clues or information in their dad's office. Junior volunteered to check the office later that day. Diamond didn't think there would be anything there, but covering all the bases was important. Diamond worked until she was famished, and then decided to grab a bite to eat.

The shrill of her cell phone ringing awakened Krystal from her sleep. "Who the hell could this be?" She grumbled before looking at the caller id. She saw it was her agent and, perked up immediately. "Cy, I hope you have good news for me."

"As a matter of fact, I do my, shining star. I've arranged the shoot for tomorrow morning at seven." Krystal jumped out of bed and told Cy, she would call him later because she had to call Dillon before he changed his mind. Krystal dialed Dillon's number and started talking before he could say hello.

"Dillon, I have great news. Cy has scheduled our shoot for seven o'clock tomorrow morning."

"I don't even get a good morning?"

"Don't give me a hard time when I called you with great news. Now you can schedule your flight to Vegas."

"That's already been scheduled. I know you didn't think I would delay being with Di to stay here and do a shoot with you?"

Krystal rolled her eyes and said, "Just answer your phone when I call you later with the rest of the details."

"You could be a little nicer since I AM doing you a huge favor."

"How many times do you want me to say thank you?"

"It's not how you say thank you. It's when you say it that gets on my last nerve."

"I'll give you a call later." Krystal pressed END without saying goodbye. Dillon irritated her.

After getting off the phone with Krystal, Dillon decided to head in to work early. As he packed up to leave, Dante stop by.

"Hey, man, what's up? Are you leaving out this early to go to the center?" Dante had on his usual black. He wore his favorite color even when it was well into the nineties.

"Yeah, man, I'm trying to tie up some loose ends before I leave for Vegas."

"That's why I'm here so early. I know Di has her hands full with her parents' case, but if you get the chance, see if she started on Phil's case. He's stressing out."

"Look, man, I'm going to tell you what I told Phil, I can't push Di. She didn't want to take the case at all. I had to put pressure on her."

"Phil isn't a woman beater. It's that crazy chick, Whitney that's got his mind all twisted."

"That's neither here or there, man. You know he put himself in this dangerous situation when he didn't listen to us. We tried to warn him about Whitney."

"Come on, man, you know the heart wants what the heart wants. Look at how long it took you to snag Di and the agony she put you through."

"Di had a career and a future that didn't involve trapping a man to be a baby daddy to four other children."

"Okay, rub it in, man. You're blessed to find a gem like Di, while we normal dudes have to be stuck with CZs."

"Hey, Di is the best thing to happen in my life. The only problem we've had since we met is her spoiled rotten baby sister."

"Man, that chick is a piece of work. I feel sorry for the unlucky fool that falls for her." Dante shook his head.

"Tell me about it. I have to do a shoot with her cranky ass in the morning."

"Man, how did you get roped into that one? I know. Don't tell me. Di laid down the law, and you caved."

"Man, shut the hell up. I run things around here. I know how, when, and where to pick my battles and this one wasn't big enough to cause my baby further stress."

"Okay, man, we've chatted long enough. Just think about the little people while you and Di are away."

"I will. I just wish this could've been the honeymoon we never had the chance to take, but until we find her parents, Di is going to work herself to the bone."

"Cheer up. You guys will get a chance to have some alone time soon and make that baby you all want so badly."

"Correction, a baby I want so badly. Di doesn't want to take time away from her career to have a baby. But she agreed to think about it because she knows how important it is to me." On that note Dillon and Dante left to get their day started.

Chapter Thirteen

"Kristinaaaa," Reggie yelled, as he raced through the front door.

"In the den, honey." Kristina called out to him.

"Sweetheart, are you okay?" Reggie asked out of breath.

The panicked look on Reggie's face made Kristina feel even worse than when she first called him. "Baby, I didn't mean for you to rush home. I just wanted…"

"Kristie, what did you think I would do when you called me and said something was going on with our baby?"

"I'm sorry, baby. I felt my first flutter and realized there's a new life growing inside of me."

"Kristie, please do not do this to me again. I almost got into two accidents flying home like a bat out of hell."

"Okay, baby. Next time I'll tell Marissa." Marissa was the nurse/companion Reggie and Nick insisted Kristina hire to ensure her pregnancy went off without a hitch.

"Well, since I'm home, I guess I should stay. Do you want anything to eat or drink?"

"No, baby, I just had two sandwiches and some chips about an hour ago."

"I didn't have lunch so I'm going to grab a bite to eat." Reggie left the room and headed to the kitchen. He was in there for a few minutes when Kristina screamed his name at the top of her lungs. Reggie dropped his plate and rushed to Kristina's side, beating Marissa by a few seconds, Kristina pointed at the television.

The bank where Reggie worked was surrounded by the police and SWAT. He turned the volume up louder. There had been an attempted robbery at the bank. The breaking news reported that the bank manager, a close friend of Reggie's had been shot to death along with two tellers, and three customers. Several others were injured in the attempted heist.

Kristina sobbed uncontrollably. "That could have been you. That could have been you." Marissa left the room to get Kristina a mild sedative, while Reggie sat next to her on the sofa, rocking her like she was a baby.

"This baby is already a Godsend, Reggie. She or he knew you were in trouble and reached out to protect you." Kristina sobbed.

"Sweetheart, you need to take it easy. I'm fine and everything worked out the way it was supposed to."

"Reggie, you couldn't have been gone more than a few minutes before the robbery happened. What about the next time? You could have easily been one of the fatalities." Kristina cried.

"Kristie, don't think like that. I'm here safe and sound with you."

Both cell phones and the house phone started ringing. Marissa must have answered the house phone because it stopped ringing. Reggie went into the living room to answer his cell, and Kristina answered hers.

"Kristie, is everything okay there? I just heard a news report about the attempted robbery at the bank," Diamond asked with concern.

"Di, calm down. Everything is fine here, thanks to your niece or nephew." Kristina explained what happened to a silent Diamond.

"God, sometimes I wished I could clone myself. I feel pulled in so many different directions to the point where I don't know whether I'm coming or going," Diamond said.

"Di, you're where you're supposed to be. Dillon will be there with you in two short days, so some of the pressure you're feeling will be lifted." Marissa brought Kristina the house phone. "Look, I gotta go. Everybody is probably worried about Reggie. You take care of yourself, Di. I'm okay." She disconnected from the call with Diamond and answered her house phone.

Dior and Krystal were both on the other end. Kristina told them the same story she told Diamond a few minutes ago, but she was beginning to feel the effects of the mild sedative Marissa gave her so she ended the call with her sisters to get some rest.

Junior had been in his dad's office for an hour when his cell phone rang. He started not to answer it, but his mom would keep calling.

"Why must you always take your sweet time answering your phone when you know it's me calling? I bet if it was the deserter or one of those hideous girls calling you would've answered sooner."

"Good evening to you too, Ma. How's your day going?"

"It would be going a lot better if you come over more often."

"Ma, I was just over there a few days ago."

"A lot could happen in a few days, Junior. Just find the deserter and his slut, they could tell you that."

"Ma, please. You said you would do better. How do you expect to have people around you if you continue to be so hateful? As it is, I'm the only constant in your life."

"I don't need those damn traitors in my life. They should've given us more support when we were left alone to fend for ourselves."

"Ma, you were really bitter back then. You drove everyone away and then blamed them for your actions and what happened between you and dad."

"Boy, don't you dare smart mouth your mother. You need to stop hanging around those disrespectful hussies you call your sisters."

"Ma, I call them my sisters because that's what they are, no matter how you feel about it. And, I'm not smart mouthing you. I'm just trying to get you to understand life would be easier if you lighten up about the past."

"You still haven't answered my question. When are you coming over here? I want to discuss my birthday plans with you."

"In that case, I'll be over in about an hour."

"This time when you come over, don't be in such a rush to leave. Every time you come over here, you rush to leave like you can't stay for more than fifteen minutes. And make sure you use your key."

"Okay, Ma. See you in a few." Junior asked his dad's assistant to lock the office, and headed out to meet his mom.

Kristina heard voices coming from downstairs. She wasn't aware of what was going on until she remembered she could've lost her husband today if it wasn't for their baby's movement. Calling Reggie to tell him about the flutters she'd felt may have saved his life. She still felt a little drowsy from the sedative, but got out of bed and freshened up. She wanted to see what all the commotion was about.

"Listen, Reggie, I know Kristie is your wife, but she is our sister and will ALWAYS be our sister. You should've let us know how upset she was, so we could've come right over," Krystal said.

"Krystal, we're here now, and Reggie called us as soon as he could. Stop giving the man a hard time," Dior said.

"Thank you, Dior, but you don't have to take up for me. It's my responsibility to take care of MY WIFE. You can be more upsetting than the situation that happened earlier today, Krystal. Please keep your voice down before you wake Kristie up." Reggie used his hands in a lowering motion.

"That's okay, baby, I'm awake. How is everyone doing?" Reggie went to the bottom of the stairs to meet Kristina. Dior and Krystal follow behind. Once they all met up in the den, Kristina was happy to see Reggie's parents and little sister were there too. Reggie's mom got up from her seat and hugged Kristina.

"Thank you so much, sweetie. You and that bundle of joy you're carrying saved my baby's life," Reggie's mother said.

"You're welcome, Mama Rosa. But, you can thank your grandchild for being so active." Kristina was so lucky to have a mother-in-law she loved.

"Okay, son, now that we know you are okay, and Kristie is okay, we're going to head home," Reggie's dad said.

Kristina looked closely at Reggie's dad. He looked tired. She hoped there wasn't anything wrong because they had their hands full already trying to have a safe pregnancy. Dior and Krystal stayed for another hour then headed home with the promise to tell Junior about the events of the day.

Chapter Fourteen

Krystal prayed the slight bags under her eyes wouldn't be noticeable during the shoot this morning. When she got back home last night from Kristina's, it was hard to fall asleep. Krystal didn't care what other people thought about her. She could think about other people's welfare. She wasn't as selfish and self-centered as people thought. She was truly worried about Kristina and hoped the drama at Reggie's job wouldn't be too much for her on top of their missing parents. Now, was the time for business. She was surprised Dillon sounded wide awake when she called to make sure he wouldn't oversleep. He told her to be on time because he had a lot to do today.

Krystal had packed everything she needed for the shoot last night. She said a silent prayer as she carried her tote and garment bag to her car. She needed everything to go well today. She drove the twenty minutes to the studio and, was happy to see Dillon already there chatting with Cy and the two New York agents when she arrived. She approached with a big smile on her face, realizing what a big accomplishment she pulled off convincing Dillon to do the shoot. Krystal gave Dillon a hug and introduced herself to the agents. She was a little jealous at how interested they were in Dillon, but she dismissed the feeling knowing they wouldn't have him there if not for her.

The group went into the room where the photo shoot would take place. The lighting was bright which made the room look sunny. Kendra, one of the agents from New York explained there would be individual and group shots. Dillon would take his individual shots first since he was under time constraints. Both Dillon and Krystal would have to change several times between shots. After Dillon finished the individual shots, they would photograph the group.

They started off with the summer collection, moved to casual wear, business wear, and ended with evening wear. Krystal wore a ball gown, and Dillon wore a matching tux. Krystal and Dillon made a striking power couple on camera. Dillon had to give Krystal her props, she was amazing at her job and her personality seemed to change when she was working. When they finished their group shots, they took a break for lunch. Krystal would do her individuals later that afternoon. Dillon started to decline lunch, but since the shoot ended a few hours early, he accepted their offer.

They went to an upscale bistro in downtown Atlanta. Right before they were about to order dessert, Dillon stood and said he had to leave. Kendra asked if he had a few minutes to chat, so he returned to his seat.

"Dillon, as you are aware, we've been after you for a long time," Cy commented.

Kendra took over, "We'd like to offer you a contract with our agency."

"We know you don't want to do this on a full-time basis any longer, so we'd like to offer you the freedom to make your own part-time schedule, and get free advertising for your youth center," Brian jumped in.

"Look, guys, I appreciate the offer. But now is really a bad time to talk about this. I'm about to go meet my wife in Vegas," Dillon said.

"We understand your position. Just give it some thought, Dillon. You don't have to decide right now. Talk it over with your wife, and we'll make it happen the way you want it to without affecting your responsibilities at the center or to your wife. We know you two are still newlyweds," Kendra added.

"Okay, I can't promise you anything right now. My mind is already in Vegas."

Dillon stood to leave, and the agents stood to shake his hand. Krystal gave him a sisterly hug. Krystal hoped they would offer her a contract similar Dillon's, but full-time.

"Okay, guys, now that Dillon is situated, what about Krystal?" Cy asked.

"We don't understand what you're asking, Cy," Kendra said

"Well, from the shoot earlier, you must know that Krystal has a talent that's a perfect fit for your agency."

"Cy, you know we have a shortage of male models, whereas female models are a dime a dozen," Brian said.

"I know that, Brian, but since the opportunity has presented itself, we wanted to let you know Krystal is interested in taking her career to the next level," Cy continued.

"Let's be frank about the matter, Cy, since you insist on bringing this up now. You know the problem with Krystal isn't her work, which is excellent. It's the drama she brings to the table," Kendra said.

"All of that was in the past. You know since I've taken over as her manager, Krystal has an excellent reputation for quality work and work ethic," Cy said.

"I tell you what," Brian said, "Let's table this conversation until after Krystal finishes her individual shots."

After enjoying dessert, the group left the bistro and went back to the studio. Krystal pouted all the way back. She was going to let Cy have it if he did not get her a contract. She would know for sure she was being used to get Dillon if he didn't. She may be young, but she'd been in this industry too many years to let anyone get away with using her. She didn't like Kendra or Brian, but they were a stepping stone to getting where she wanted. She would know she made it when people like them were begging for her time.

Chapter Fifteen

Junior thought over his conversations with his mom and wife last night. He realized both women were selfish and ungrateful. He visited with his mom for almost two hours before they came up with something solid for her birthday. They were having a good conversation until Junior mentioned he wanted to make sure Jalissa and Joe didn't make any other plans that would conflict with her birthday plans.

"Why do they have to be a part of my special day? Shouldn't I be the one to decide how I want to spend my birthday?"

"Ma, you need to stop this right now. I've had it with you treating my wife and son like they don't matter."

"I didn't say they don't matter, I was thinking we could have a nice dinner then go to a play or something."

"Ma, I want to do more than that for you. Besides, auntie and her family want to join us."

"Don't mention that traitor and her brood to me. "I don't want to be around those heathens."

"Ma, they're going to help pay for whatever we decide to do. Your sister loves you and so does the rest of her family, so lighten up."

"That's the second time you said that to me. I refuse to be around someone who didn't see fit to help us when we needed it."

"Ma, you were so evil. I remember many times when Auntie tried to reason with you, but you ignored her or threw her out of our house."

"I was the injured party, and she had the damn nerve to stay friends with the deserter for a little while after he left us. Now, what kind of sister would treat her family like that?"

"Ma, let's talk about something else. What did you do today to keep yourself busy?"

"I spent most of the day missing my damn programs because some fools decided to rob a bank instead of getting a job, and regular programs were preempted."

"That's sad, Ma. All you could think about were your programs when a tragedy like that happened."

"Why should I care? My money isn't in that bank and even if it was, it would be insured."

"Was anyone hurt, Ma?"

"The deserter banks there so why should I care at all what happened at that damn bank?"

"Oh my God, you mean to tell me this incident happened at National Savings and Loans? Kristie's husband, Reggie works at that bank."

"Why the hell do you continue to bring those creatures, names up to me, like I care about any of them?"

"Ma, what do you want to do for your birthday?" Junior pulled his phone out to call Kristina and noticed the missed texts from Dior and Diamond. Both said all was well, and they would talk to him tomorrow.

"What's the rush? Are you trying to rush out of here to see what's happening with the creatures?"

"Okay, I see you don't have a sense of humor tonight. I was thinking it's time for me to take a vacation, so that's what I want to do for my birthday. Take a trip away from here."

"Where and when would you like to go on your trip, Ma?" Junior was glad to be getting off so easy. Now, he didn't have to worry about all the drama it would be to have all of his family

together. He had enough to worry about dealing with his dad and stepmom's disappearance.

"Well, I was thinking I would like to go the Bahamas."

"Okay, Ma, when do you want to go and for how long, so we can start making plans?" Junior should have known she would pick someplace extravagant. Jalissa was going to have a fit.

"I think a week would be sufficient."

"Okay, Ma, Jalissa and I will pay for the flight and hotel stay, and whatever money we get from the rest of the family, you can use for spending money."

"Okay, now you can leave so I can get my beauty rest, I'm beat."

"Talk to you tomorrow. I love you, Ma."

"Love you too, baby. I'm glad you stayed for a while and didn't rush out of here like you normally do."

"Goodnight, Ma." Junior gave his mom a hug and headed home.

When Junior got home twenty minutes later and told Jalissa about his mom's plans for her birthday, she went ballistic."

"Where the hell do you think we're going to get that kind of money from to pay for that trip?"

"Come on, honey. This is a special birthday for her. She deserves to get away and enjoy herself."

"She can get away all she wants, but not on our dime. We have things we need to take care of and spending that kind of money on your evil ass mom isn't going to cut it."

"We can afford to send her on this trip, so why are you acting like we can't?"

"You know damn well why I'm acting like this. That woman treats me and our son like dirt, and you expect me to spend my hard-earned money on her? NOT GOING TO HAPPEN," Jalissa said.

"Listen, I'm getting sick and tired of both of you acting like damn kids. Grow the hell up and think about someone else besides yourselves. I'm tired of being stuck in the middle of y'all hateful asses."

"You need to stop all that yelling before you wake Joe up. I'm a grown ass woman, Junior, and I will continue to speak my mind about things that are bothering me."

"Speak your mind all you want, but I WILL NOT put up with either yours or mom's childish behaviors any longer."

"Who are you calling childish? I'm not the one begging for my parents' approval. Do what you, want, you always do when it comes to those people."

"I don't beg anyone for anything. Just because I care about my parents' feelings doesn't make me childish and stop calling them those people. Can we talk about something else? I think it's time for me to switch gears and do something more productive with my professional life," Junior said.

"Wow, about time. What were you thinking about doing?"

"Well, helping the girls with the search for Dad and Mama Beth made me realize how much I like investigative work. When I was at the firm today, I even went as far as picking out an office."

"Oh, I guess that would be better than the work you've been doing."

"Come on, baby. You don't like my idea?" Junior hadn't liked the disappointed look on his wife's face.

"It's alright, but I thought you would do something more corporate."

"You know that's not me. I'm in my element doing this type of work. Let's sleep on it and talk about it tomorrow."

"What did your mom have to say about your decision?"

"She was happy until I told her the reason why I wanted to go into this profession." Junior and Jalissa had stayed up another hour talking before they turned in for the night. Looking back on that conversation Junior realized he should've told Jalissa he wanted to go to Vegas to help Diamond with the case.

Chapter Sixteen

Diamond couldn't believe her eyes when she woke up and looked into the eyes of her husband. She had told the front desk Dillon would arrive sometime this afternoon and to give him a key to her room. She glanced over at the clock. It was barely seven in the morning.

"Oh my God, you're a sight for sore eyes. I didn't expect you until later this afternoon."

"Enough talking, we can do that later," Dillon said.

Later came at two o'clock in the afternoon when they ordered room service.

"You better not tell her this, but I got to see a gentler and kinder side of Krystal during the shoot. She was actually likable."

"Wow, that's amazing. I knew she had it in her to be a better person. I just hope she keeps her promise to help out with the case."

"That girl was really impressive. I can see why she's in demand. If she changes her attitude towards life and how she treats people, she would get even farther in her career. She may even be the next Tyra Banks."

"Thank you for doing the shoot, baby. I know you wanted to leave that life behind."

"It wasn't that bad, and I kind of enjoyed it. As a matter of fact, the agents from New York offered me a part-time contract and said I would be able to do all the work in Atlanta."

"Wow, that's great, baby. What did you tell them?"

"I told them I would have to talk to the boss lady. The only reason I would consider it is to get exposure for the center."

"What about Krystal? Was she offered a contract?"

"Not while I was there, but since she has an agent and still had to do her individual shots, they may have wanted to wait to talk to her after that."

"Well, I hope they offer her something. If they don't that would give her a reason to have a bigger chip on her shoulder."

Dillon tucked a strand of hair behind Diamond's ear. "Enough talk on that subject. Wasn't that some weird shit that happened with Reggie and Kristie?"

"Yes, it was. Imagine being saved by someone that's not even born yet. Kristie would've been devastated if Reggie were there and had been injured or killed."

"I just hope she doesn't be so scared for him that every time he leaves the house or goes to work she panics."

Diamond shook her head. "That won't happen. She would be concerned, but she isn't as fragile as people think. It's just this time with her pregnancy, they want to be careful so what happened before won't happen again."

"And speaking of pregnancy, I was going to wait until I got back home before I brought this up, but since we're talking about it I might as well tell you now. I think I'm pregnant." The blank look on Dillon's face surprised Diamond.

"What did you say, Di?"

"I said I think I'm pregnant. I took two pregnancy tests and both were positive."

"But, you said you wanted to wait another year or so before we tried."

"I know, but I thought it would be cool if our baby and Kristie's were close in age. Plus, I didn't want to get your hopes up if I had problems conceiving."

"Oh my God, Di, I've wanted this for so long, but I knew you weren't ready, so I didn't want to push you." Tears swelled in Dillon's eyes.

"Well, I stopped taking birth control in November hoping I could give you a special Christmas gift, but that didn't happen. When I got here, I was sluggish, but I thought it was because of my parents' situation. Then I remembered I was late, so I bought a test the day after I got here and another one yesterday to be sure."

Dillon grabbed Diamond and kissed her. She hoped she wasn't jumping the gun by telling Dillon before she went to see a doctor. Dillon was on cloud nine, but Diamond convinced him not to tell his family about the baby until she went to the doctor to make sure the two pregnancy tests weren't a mistake. Dillon agreed to wait until she saw a doctor, but said that first thing in the morning they would be seeing a doctor in Vegas instead of waiting until they got back home.

They decided to have an early dinner before they started on the information Diamond had gathered so far. She wanted to introduce Dillon to Mr. Pittman and the two detectives working the case.

Dillon had good instincts about people, and she wanted to see if he shared her impression about Mr. Pittman.

Diamond called the front desk to see if Mr. Pittman was working. The desk clerk said he wouldn't be in until six o'clock, so Diamond and Dillon decided to do some sight-seeing until Mr. Pittman started his shift.

Krystal was still livid from yesterday's meeting with the New York agents. Kendra had done most of the talking, but Brian seemed to agree with whatever she said. Cy had to promise that Krystal would be on her best behavior and still they only offered her a short-term contract with an out clause if she didn't act appropriately. There wasn't a set date for her to start since she was on leave until her parents were located.

Krystal still couldn't get over the fact they were falling all over Dillon who had been out of the business for years and didn't want to return while she worked all the time and wanted a contract badly. She could hear Diamond telling her this would happen if she didn't get her act together. She decided to call Cy to let him know how she felt about the situation.

"Cy, you know that was bullshit how they treated me yesterday, and you didn't do anything to smooth things over."

"Good morning, shining star. How are you on this blessed morning?"

"Don't blessed morning me. Why didn't you push harder to get me a better contract? What am I paying you for if you can't get me a decent contract?"

"You have your foot in the door and that's all you need to prove yourself," Cy said.

"I've proven myself for years. I shouldn't have to scramble for a contract with someone as cranky and rude as Kendra Kerr and her lapdog Brian Jemison."

"Let's enjoy our blessings, shining star, and if we're lucky enough to get Dillon to do more work that would work out in your favor."

"I shouldn't have to depend on Dillon to get a decent contract. I've worked my butt off for my own rewards."

"Come on, shining star, you've been in this business long enough to know it takes more than talent and skills to climb the success ladder. You also have to have the ability to work and get along with others. Most people see it as bull-shitting, but that's the way of the world in this industry."

"Whatever, Cy. My diva tendencies and I have to go and get our day started. I have to prove to my family they can count on me, which is irritating because they expect me to change overnight. And now that damn Kendra Kerr wants me to prove to her that I'm easy to work with. To hell with all of you." Krystal didn't wait for a response from Cy, she ended their call.

Chapter Seventeen

Reggie decided to take a week off from work after the incident at the bank. The grandparents refused to take Reggie or Kristina's word that she was okay. Now they all sat in Reggie and Kristina's dining room along with Krystal, Junior, and Denise.

"Family, Kristie and I appreciate your love and support, but everything is good," Reggie said.

"We don't mean to be a bother, but we had to see for ourselves that both of you are okay," Nick's dad said.

"We also wanted to know if there was any news. How come they haven't found my baby yet?" Bethany's mother asked.

"You guys are not a bother. And Grandma Stacey, I'm sure Di will have some news for us soon," Reggie said.

"We should have information soon. Dillon and our investigative team from the firm are in Vegas with Di now, and I'll be going out there next week," Junior said.

"How could you ask me to help out with the case and then leave town? I know you don't expect me to go to Vegas with you." Krystal rolled her neck. "The last thing I need in my life right now is Di's criticism. I knew I shouldn't have taken time off from work."

"Little girl, if one more smart-ass comment come out of your selfish ass mouth, I will slap you silly and throw you out of this house myself," Krystal's Aunt Denise said.

Everyone was flabbergasted, looking from Denise to Krystal. Krystal was shocked by her aunt's aggressive words and couldn't think of what to say.

"That's enough. I can't have this kind of behavior upsetting my wife," Reggie said.

"That wasn't necessary, Auntie. You aren't the only one worried about Mom and Dad. And, I will continue to speak my mind no matter what anyone thinks." Krystal folded her arms. "Besides, I'm not complaining, I was just stating that I don't want to go to Vegas. I still want to help out with the case."

Reggie cleared his throat. "I really appreciate you all coming over. Feel free to stay as long as you like, but Kristie needs to rest. She's been up all morning, and even though it's good that everyone is over here, this is a little too much for her right now." Reggie was about to take Kristina to upstairs.

"Reggie, if it's okay with you, Eunice and I would like to take Kristie for her nap," Stacey said.

"That's a great idea honey. I would like to spend a little time with my grandmothers," Kristina said.

"Okay, Kristie. As long as you get some rest. I will stay and entertain the rest of the family," Reggie told his wife.

"I want to come too," Krystal said,

"Krystal, we need you to stay here and let Kristie spend some alone time with the grandmothers." There was no way Reggie wanted Krystal to invoke her bad attitude on his wife.

With an attitude, Krystal said, "Fine, I'll just stay here."

Once Kristina and the grandmothers left the room, Denise said, "I know there's something we can do from here to help with the search."

"I agree, Reggie said. "I know Kristie would want to help out in some way with the search."

"Okay. When I get home, I'll check with Di and put together a list before I leave for Vegas," Junior offered.

"I can't see where there's anything to do from this end. Since Di, Dillon, and the investigative team are working in Vegas, that should cover everything," Krystal said.

"Krystal, let's see what Junior and Di can put together. I know there's something we can do to help like Auntie Niecy said, even if it's just making phone calls," Reggie said, before escorting everyone into the family room since they weren't ready to leave. .

Diamond and Dillon sat in the waiting room at Vegas On Call Urgent Care. Diamond had mixed feelings. She wanted a baby, but she knew if she was pregnant, Dillon would smother her and make her take it easy. Her work was very important to her, and with her parents missing, there was no way she was going to stop until she got to the bottom of what happened to them.

While she waited, she thought about their meeting last night with the unnerving hotel manager. Mr. Pittman seemed to have a new attitude with Dillon present. He was careful with his words and tried to be more accommodating. Little did he know, Diamond would eat him up and spit him out quicker than Dillon. She and Dillon were scheduled to meet with the detectives later, and then they planned to visit the other hotels. Diamond felt like they were finally making some progress.

"Diamond Washington." The nurse's assistant call Diamond's name.

Diamond grabbed Dillon's hand and followed the assistant into the doctor's office when she heard her name called. The assistant seated them in front of the doctor's desk.

"Congratulations, Mr. and Mrs. Washington, you're pregnant," The doctor said.

Dillon jumped out of his chair and danced around the room. He picked up Diamond and gave her a big hug and kiss. Diamond smiled when she saw the ecstatic look on Dillon's face.

"We won't do a pelvic exam here, Mrs. Washington. Just make sure you follow up with your primary care doctor, so you can begin this pregnancy off on a good foot. Now what questions can I answer for you?"

Before leaving the doctor's office, Diamond and Dillon asked tons of questions. Then they went to celebrate the confirmation of Diamond's pregnancy with breakfast.

Chapter Eighteen

Atlanta

Junior sat on the loveseat next to Jalissa massaging her feet. Joe was at Jalissa's parents' house for the next two weeks, so they were alone.

Junior cleared his throat.

"Jay, baby, I have something important to talk to you about."

"I don't like the sound of that, Junior. What have you gotten yourself into this time?"

"Jay, don't be like that. The search for Dad and Mama Beth isn't going well. I want to go to Vegas next week to help."

"What the hell do you think you can do that Diamond, Dillon, or the investigative team isn't already doing? The shit you've come up with lately is driving me crazy. First, you want to spend tons of money on somebody that treats me and your son like dirt, and now you want to travel hundreds of miles away wasting your time." Jalissa looked at Junior like he had grown two heads.

"Come on, baby. I told you this is the field I want to get into. What better way than to assist with this case? Plus, it's another way to prove to Dad that I'm serious about improving my professional life."

"So, I'm supposed to stay here alone with Joe gone over to my parents for the next two weeks? How long are you planning on being gone?"

"Hopefully, we can find them soon, so I won't have to be gone too long. But to answer your question, I don't know exactly how long I'll be gone."

"Honey bunch, what's going on with us? Our lack of communication is beginning to scare me. You know I'm very happy you decided to do something more productive with your life, but I didn't expect it to take you so far away from me and Joe."

"I know, baby. But when we find Dad and Mama Beth, I'll be able to make amends with Dad and prove to him I can be more than a drifter."

"You mean he had the nerve to call you a drifter?" You see, that's what I'm talking about. Since I've known you, he has always put you down while he keeps those girls on a pedestal, especially, that bratty ass Krystal." Jalissa slapped her palms against her thighs. "See, this is what I don't understand. How in the world did you turn out so sane with a dead-beat dad and a deranged mom?"

"Jalissa stop. You know I've given my dad plenty of reasons to be frustrated with me. I just have to rebuild his trust in me again. It's not just about the money because I know if I pushed hard enough I could get all of my trust fund. I want Dad to know I'm ready to step up to the plate and take my rightful place in the family as the oldest child."

"Good luck with that one. Di has that place on lockdown, and she has it all brains, beauty, and most importantly, a very strong work ethic. You know how much that means to your old man."

"It's not a contest, Jay. There's room at the top for both of us since it's just Di and I that want to work with Dad."

"I'll give it to Di, Dior, Kristie, and maybe even Ms. Beth. They've always tried to include me and Joe as part of the family. I can accept them giving me the cold shoulder, but not my baby." Jalissa's eyes welled with tears.

"In light of all that's happened, I'm sure the family will make more of an effort to get along. We've even gotten Krystal to lighten up a little. Of course, she's still a work in progress, but I can see she's trying harder. Struggling, but trying."

"Well, I'm not going to beg anyone to accept me or Joe, but I am willing to make an effort if they're willing to do the same."

Junior hugged Jalissa. "I love you, baby. Why don't we plan to do something special before I leave, and maybe you could schedule a girl's night for next Saturday with your girls. You could even invite my sisters."

Hmmm, I actually like that idea. I'll call Dior and Kristie to see if they could join me and the girls, honey bunch. Just make sure you don't stay away too long."

"Aren't you forgetting someone?"

"No," Jalissa shook her head. "I'll ask Dior to ask that little demon about coming over. I hope she's on her best behavior. I want this to be about fun, since everyone is so stressed out."

"Just give her a chance, Jay."

Diamond and Dillon left the police station with little to no information. The detectives continued to stonewall them, refusing to divulge the name of the hotels the other missing couples were registered at. The detectives would only say that the families of the other missing couples were also anxious to find their loved ones. Diamond refused to be placated. She and Dillon decided to visit the hotel on both sides of Caesars Palace. It seemed like it would be a waste of time visiting the second hotel after not having any luck with the first. As they were about to leave, an off-duty desk clerk asked them to meet her in the lobby area in the corner in ten minutes. Once she joined them, she started whispering.

"I overheard you guys asking about suspicious activities and missing couples," The clerk said.

Diamond handed the clerk a business card. "I'm Diamond Morgan-Washington, and this is my husband, Dillon. And yes, my parents have been missing for a week. We've been searching for them, but no one will give us any answers. They were staying at Caesars Palace."

"There's been a lot of that going around lately, but no one wants to get involve."

"Well, somebody better get involved. I'm not leaving here without my parents. I know there's a lot more going on than what we've been told. Do you have any idea how we can get in touch with the other families?" Diamond asked.

"Shhh," the clerk looked around. "I could lose my job for this. There are three couples missing from this hotel. And from what I overheard you say about your parents, it sounds like they all have similar characteristics--older, well off, on vacation from another city. And it seems like all the couples attended the same tours."

"What tours?" Dillon interjected. "Please, mam, just tell us what you know. We need some answers. I can't keep having my wife and family stressed out about this."

"The Art Exhibits and the Mob Tours. They're the most popular, but that's all I can tell you. The clerk walked away as quickly as she had appeared.

Diamond's mouth dropped open. "What the hell is going on around here?"

Chapter Nineteen

Nick woke up with a monster headache. He didn't have a clue where he was. His mouth was dry, and his stomach was growling. Then, it came back to him. He was in the same place he had been for days, and refused to eat or drink until he saw his wife. All he could think about was Bethany and his family and friends back in Atlanta. He hadn't seen his wife since the day they were tricked on that tour she didn't want to go on in the first place. Now Nick wished he had listened to her when she told him something wasn't right, but he thought making new acquaintances with the other eight couples from their hotel and the two adjourning hotels would be good for them.

Nick had told Bethany they needed some adventure, but he hadn't bargained for this. Nick still didn't know what was going on, and his legal mind wouldn't stop working. The host had said no ransom was involved. Why were they being held if money wasn't the motive? And why were they kept separate from their wives?

Nick and the other captives who were also attorneys asked tons of questions, although they didn't get any answers. He knew their family and friends had to be worried sick about them. The last person Nick had conversed with was his best friend Vincent.

"Man, I can't believe I'm letting this woman talk me into going on this sissy ass art exhibit tour,"

"Suck it up, chump. You know you've never been able to say no to Beth. Besides, didn't she promise to go on that Al Capone mystery tour with you?"

"For your information, it isn't Al Capone. It's a Private Mob Tour that has nothing to do with that dude."

"Either way, you know she doesn't like spooky things. It's a test of her love for you that she's willing to go anyway."

"Whatever, man, I forgot how whipped you are."

"I think we're in the same boat on that one, my friend."

"Ok, man. I better hang up now before my darling wife hog tie me for keeping her waiting."

"Just think today is for her and tomorrow is for you. What better way to show your love for each other than a compromise?"

"Well, when we finish with that tour of torture, we can relax the rest of the day and get ready for the real fun tomorrow."

Nick groaned. Exactly how many days ago had that been?

Bethany took a look around the room and wondered where she was and why. The host said she wanted them to bond over the things they had in common, but Bethany didn't feel she had anything in common with any of these women. Even though there were different races and ethnic backgrounds represented, most of them looked like they were born into money.

Bethany's family didn't come from money. Bethany was worried about so many things, but most of all her husband and children. She hadn't seen Nick in days, and she still didn't have a clear memory as to how they had gotten separated.

The girls and Junior must be worried sick about them. The last thing Kristina needed was stress. This pregnancy was so important to all of them. Bethany didn't know how Kristina or the rest of the family would get though another miscarriage. They all wanted Kristina to be extra careful.

Bethany had a feeling the girls and Junior would rally together to find out what happened to her and Nick, but she wished it would not take a situation like this to bring them closer together. She smiled thinking about how Krystal was probably driving them all crazy. Outside of herself, Nick, and Dior, no one else was able handle Krystal and her misguided behaviors. To tell the truth, Dior was better at it than Bethany and Nick. Bethany was so into her thoughts, she didn't hear the host asking her a question. Instead of answering, she turned her head the other way. Bethany prayed this would all be over soon.

Chapter Twenty

"Krystal, Jalissa wants the three of us to come over to her house and spend the night next Saturday, along with a few of her friends since Junior and Joe will be away. It's going to be sort of a girls' night," Dior said.

"You know she doesn't want me to come. She knew she couldn't invite you and Kristie without inviting me." Krystal frowned.

"Baby girl, how about we try to make amends and be a united family for once? When Mom and Dad get back home, it would be nice for them to return to a family that isn't at each other throats?"

"Dior, do you think Mom and Dad are still alive?"

"I don't know," Dior shrugged her shoulders. "Sometimes I feel they are, but then other times, my mind wonders about what happened to them. It must be tragic since they haven't contacted anyone for so long."

"Well, I just hope we find out something one way or the other, because the unknown is about to drive me crazy."

"That's why I think it's a good idea to go over to Jalissa's next week. We need to take our mind off all of this for a little while.

Who knows? This may be the push we need to become close as a family."

"Okay, I'll go, but that ghetto woman better not even think about starting any shit with me."

"That works both ways, baby girl. Try to be nice to her for a change."

It took Kristina over a half hour to convince Reggie into letting her go over to Jalissa's for the girls' night. She knew the only reason he agreed was because Dior would be there to put a stop to any commotion Jalissa or Krystal may start. Reggie didn't care for Jalissa because she always tried to act like Junior's mother instead of his wife.

"Thank you for being so understanding, baby. Maybe you can get with your boys or visit your parents and baby sister. I know they would love to spend more time with you after what happened at the bank," Kristina said.

"I'll think about it. I may stay home and do some work on me and Jr.'s man cave."

"I don't think our daughter would like your man cave. Maybe you should hold off on making too many changes with that in mind."

"At this point, I don't care what sex our child is as long as both of you are healthy," Reggie said.

"Amen to that. Now come and help me pack for next week's girl's night so I can be ready when Dior and Krystal come to get me. You know how impatient Krystal can get at times."

Jalissa arranged the entertainment room to her liking, before going into the kitchen to check on the appetizers. She called to make sure the food was on schedule. She had thought about cooking dinner herself, but decided against it since she would be cooking breakfast in the morning. Only she and Krystal would not be attending church in the morning. By the time Jalissa finished tidying the house, it was time to get ready for her guests. She expected Junior's sisters to arrive first and her two best friends about an hour later. Jalissa showered and dressed in a simple, bright red lounge dress. As soon as she stepped on the bottom stair, the doorbell rang. She put on the best smile she could muster and opened the door to greet her sisters-in-law. Dior and Kristina gave her a big hug, but Krystal barely touched her, which did not make one bit of difference to Jalissa.

"Come on in, ladies. We can sit in the living room while we wait for my girlfriends to arrive. Would y'all like a snack?" Jalissa looked over her shoulder at Junior's sisters as they followed her through the house.

"We would love that. Thank you." Kristina spoke for the group."

"Girl, it smells good in here. I can't wait to sample whatever it is I smell," Dior said.

"Oh! Look at us on your wall. I can't believe that was two years ago. Dior, look." Kristina said, as the sisters' oooed and ahhed over the family pictures of them blown up from two Christmases ago.

"Hmph, I can't believe she has pictures of us on her wall," Krystal said.

"Why not?" Jalissa asked, returning from the kitchen with a tray of hors d oeuvres and drinks. She set the tray down and waited for Krystal to answer.

"Krystal," Dior said.

"Nah, its okay, Dior." Jalissa waved her hand. "Y'all are Junior's family. Even if you don't like me and my son, why wouldn't I have my husband's family on our wall in our family home?"

Ding Dong. "Excuse me, that must be Fallon and Kimberly." Jalissa went to answer the door.

"Krystal!" Dior and Kristina said at the same time.

"What?" Krystal asked, stuffing a piece of fruit into her mouth.

Jalissa's two best friends entered the living room, diffusing the tension. Jalissa introduced everyone and asked them to follow her downstairs.

The women walked in to a spread. There was something for everybody - Soul Food, Mexican, Chinese, and Thai. While the women ate, Jalissa kicked off the evening with an ice breaker. Each woman was asked to describe what they would like to be doing in the next year or two.

Since Krystal was the youngest in the group, Jalissa asked her to start.

"I would like to be in New York or maybe Los Angles making people like Kendra Kerr and Brian Jemison beg me to work with them," Krystal said explaining who Kendra and Brian were.

"Maybe it's a good thing they're being cautious right now. That way when you are working with the big-time agents and companies, you'll be more equipped to handle them by starting out at a slow pace," Jalissa said.

"I've been in this industry over ten years. I shouldn't have to prove myself. I'm good at what I do. No. I take that back, I'm great," Krystal said smugly.

"Baby girl, I think what Jalissa is trying to say is that starting off with little steps will give you the opportunity to wet your feet and prove yourself even more to the big-time agents," Dior added.

Jalissa nodded her head in agreement. She was determined to do right by her husband and keep the peace with his bratty ass sister.

"I'll give those fools six months at the most, but if I'm not moving in the direction of high fashion modeling, I'm getting rid of all three of their sorry behinds."

"I'll go next. Once my baby is around six months, I plan to focus on finishing my degree and deciding what home-based business I want to start. I want to have the best of both worlds, like my mom, where I can stay at home with my family and fulfill my personal dreams," Kristina said.

"I feel the same way, but my road dogs here think I lost my mind not wanting to work outside of home." Fallon pointed to Jalissa and Kim.

"We don't think you're crazy, Fallon. We just don't want you to have any regrets that you didn't pursue a career outside of the home," Kim said.

"Whatever, Kim, I've listened to this speech so many times over the years, I hear it in my sleep. Kristina, don't let anyone make you feel bad about wanting to be a stay at home mom if that is what you truly desire. As long as you and your husband are fine with it, you shouldn't worry about what others think. Since I agree with

Kristina, and she has said what I basically wanted to say, I'll pass the floor to the next person," Fallon said.

"I'll go next. I want to open my own day-care center one day. I've been working on a business plan to present to my dad and other potential investors," Dior said.

"Wow, Dior, I didn't know you still wanted to do that. You hadn't mentioned it lately. Sign me up. I would love to be an investor," Krystal said.

"Me too, Reg and I would love to help anyway we can," Kristina offered.

"Junior and I are limited as to the amount of money we can invest, but we would love to do whatever else you need to get started," Jalissa added.

"Thank you, guys, I've been thinking about this for a while now, but with the situation with Mom and Dad...they are my main focus right now," Dior said tearfully.

"Well, I guess it's just you and I left, Kim. Do you want to go first?" Jalissa asked.

"Hmm, I've never really thought about making future plans or goals until recently, so I don't have must to share at this time. I do know as a breast cancer survivor and having come close to death more than once over the last few years, I plan to live each day to the fullest." Kim said.

"That's great, Kim." Jalissa reached over and squeezed her friend's hand. "Okay, well, I'll end this by saying, my greatest wish for now and in the near future is to be closer to my husband's family, because life is too short to hold grudges."

The women all agreed and got ready to play the first game of the night. Jalissa smiled to herself. This wasn't such a bad idea after all.

Chapter Twenty-One

Junior made it to Vegas around one-thirty in the afternoon. Atlanta time. He called Jalissa to let her know he made it safely, but she sounded distracted. She said she had just finished double checking her preparations for girl's night and told him she would call him before she went to bed. Junior checked into his room and called Diamond.

"Guess where I'm at, sis?"

"Are you already here, Junior?"

"Yep, downstairs in the lobby waiting for you guys to come down and take me to breakfast. I'm starved."

"Give us fifteen minutes and we'll meet you in the lobby."

While Junior waited on Diamond and Dillon, he decided to review some of the things he had jotted down on the plane ride. He could not wait to see the information Di had collected. The mysterious disappearance of six or more couples in broad daylight with no ransom demand frightened Junior. Since money wasn't the motivation, it was hard to determine what was going on in Sin City.

As soon as he jotted down his last thoughts, Diamond and Dillon came over to him. Almost two weeks had passed since he had last seen Diamond, and she had a glow about her that she didn't have before she left. Junior thought Dillon was the reason, but he also hoped it was because she found some new information to bring them closer to solving the case.

"Big brother, how the hell are you? It's so good to see you."

"Good, sis. What's this glow about you? I bet it has something to do with this guy here, or have you received news on Dad and Mama Beth whereabouts?"

"No, we haven't received any additional information," Diamond answered.

"Man, not the news I was hoping to hear," Junior said.

Dillon clasped Junior's shoulder. "How about we go to this eatery around the corner, and Di can bring you up to speed while we grab a bite to eat? It will be good to eat outside the hotel. We've been mostly living on room service."

The trio settled in a booth at the eatery, and Diamond said, "Well, this morning our investigative team will work with the detectives on the case. They'll also be doing more footwork checking to see what the motive of the disappearances could be since money doesn't seem to be the reason."

"That's good. I'd like to shadow them to learn a few tricks of the trade, and I may be able to offer some personal insight as well," Junior said.

Before they came down to meet with Junior, Diamond had asked Dillon if she could tell him about the baby since he was there. "Now might not be the right time for this, but Dillon and I are going to have a baby," Diamond said excitedly.

"Oh my God, that's great news. I know both of you are so happy. Now Kristie's baby will have a playmate. I've been trying to get Jalissa to have another baby, but she said that ship has sailed."

"Sorry to hear that, man, but at least you have your son," Dillon said.

"All isn't lost. She hasn't had her tubes tied, so there's a slim chance she'll change her mind," Junior said.

"We need you to keep this to yourself for now. We want to wait until we get back home before we tell the rest of the family. It's going to be hard for me to keep this from Kristie and equally hard for Dillon not to tell his parents," Diamond said.

After breakfast, the trio went back to the hotel and gathered all the materials and notes on the case from Diamond and Dillon's room and met in the hotel's business center. They were grateful to be the only ones in there, so they could talk freely.

"We have to find out what's going on sooner rather than later. Every day that passes, Dad and Mama Beth's chances of a safe return grows slimmer," Junior said.

"I know. I'm not getting a good feeling about this, but I don't feel like they are hurt or..." Diamond trailed off.

Junior thought for a few minutes and said, "So far, there's a whole lot of nothing in this report. I sure hope there's more meat in the remainder of the report. I guess we better keep digging."

Jalissa was happy about how things turned out last night. They all had fun getting to know each other, and she even saw a different side to Krystal. When she told Junior, he was shocked to hear his wife speak so kindly of his baby sister. Jalissa reminisced about last night's activities.

The first game of the night the women played was Charades. Jalissa didn't get on the team with her home-girls because she felt it wouldn't be fair for all the sisters to be on the same team, so she asked two of them to be on her team. Krystal shocked her by volunteering her and Kristina. She said the other team wouldn't stand a chance if she and Dior were on the same team.

Jalissa's team won three out of the five games. Before they played the other two games Jalissa had planned, she asked the women if there were any games they would like to play. When they said no, she introduced the next two games, Mafia and Psychiatrist.

The Mafia card game was played by selecting a leader while the remaining players formed a circle. After taking out three of the four queens, kings, and aces, a deck of cards were shuffled. Jalissa was the leader so she handed everyone in the circle a card and told them to make sure they didn't tell anyone else what card they received. She explained to the players the person with the queen was the doctor, the one with the king the cop, and the person with the ace was the Mafia.

After they looked at their cards, they gave them back to Jalissa and had to close their eyes. Jalissa called Mafia and directed that player to open her eyes and point out the answer.

When Kristina opened her eyes, Jalissa asked, "Who do you want to kill?" Kristina looked terrified because she did not want to kill anyone, but she silently pointed to Kim to be the victim. Kristina was instructed to close her eyes again.

Next, Jalissa directed the cop to open her eyes. Fallon opened her eyes, and Jalissa asked, "Who do you think the Mafia is?" Fallon silently pointed to Krystal. Jalissa instructed Fallon to close her eyes.

Next, Jalissa directed the doctor to open her eyes. When Krystal opened her eyes, Jalissa asked, "Who do you want to save?" Krystal silently pointed to Kristina. Kristina was saved, and Krystal was instructed to close her eyes.

Jalissa asked everyone to open their eyes. When they did, she announced that the Mafia killed Kim and the doctor didn't save her, so she was out of the game. Next, Jalissa asked everyone to guess who they thought was the Mafia. After a lengthy discussion, they voted and killed the person they thought was the Mafia, but they didn't win because they voted and killed Krystal. Kristina was the last woman standing, and the rest of the group was shocked to find out she was the Mafia.

Everyone enjoyed this game, but it was long and exhausting, so they were so glad the last game was short. The object of this game was to confuse the psychiatrist. Dior was chosen as the leader and sent out of the room while the remainder of the group formed a circle. They had to come up with a problem the entire group agreed upon. Once they decided on the problem, Dior was brought back into the room to ask questions of everyone in the group until she guessed the problem. After a half hour with no success, they called it a draw, which did not sit well with Dior, especially since they would not tell her what the problem was even when the game was over.

Everyone was exhausted after the games so Jalissa showed the sisters where they would be sleeping for the night. When the sisters went to bed, the JFK team (Jalissa, Fallon, and Kim) stayed behind to catch up and clean up from the night's events.

Chapter Twenty-Two

Diamond worked with Dillon and Junior reviewing all the information they had gathered since the investigation began. After a few hours, they had more questions than answers. The report from Mr. Pittman didn't help at all. Diamond had arranged to meet with their investigative team after dinner, but after reviewing the information with no success, Dillon and Junior told Diamond to go back to the room and get some rest. Diamond thought they were trying to get rid of her and didn't want to be treated like a child, but she realized how exhausted she was and took them up on their suggestion.

When they were alone, Dillon said, "Man this is some messed up shit. We've got to get some answers real quick so we can go home."

"I know, Jalissa wasn't too happy with me for leaving, especially since Joe is at her parents."

"We've been sitting back waiting for the police and the hotel management to get to the bottom of this and it's not working. I think it's up to us to light a fire under everyone involved in the investigation," Dillon said.

"I'm all for that. Let's touch base with our investigative team to see what they have gathered so far."

"Man, I want to put more pressure on the detectives. I feel like they are keeping too much from us about what's really going on."

"Since, Di will be resting for a while, why don't we go and pay them a visit?" Junior suggested.

"I'm down with that idea. While we are at it, I want to see if we can get in touch with that clerk at the other hotel. I think we can get more answers from her than those two tight-lipped dudes."

"Isn't it kind of suspicious how she approached you and Di out of the blue?"

"Man, we were so anxious for some answers, we didn't even think about why she singled us out." Dillon rubbed his face before continuing. "We probably do need to grill her a little harder, but I think it's time for the detectives to cough up some information." Dillon and Junior headed down to the precinct to see the detectives.

When the girls came down to eat breakfast the next morning, they were surprised to see everything already set up buffet style in the dining room. Kimberly and Fallon were sitting at the table while Jalissa gathered coffee and tea from the kitchen. The women ate and made small talk and everyone thanked Jalissa for all the trouble she went through to put everything together.

Jalissa stood to clear the table, but Kristina stopped her. "Sis, we can do that. You guys handled the clean up last night. Dior, Krystal and I can take care of it this morning."

"Kristie, I didn't sign up to be a maid. I have to get back home so I can light a fire under Cy to get me a better contract," Krystal said.

"Krystal, I think it's only fair that we clean this morning," Kristina insisted.

"Come on, guys. This has been a wonderful and pleasant experience, don't mess it up with your arguing," Dior said.

"It's no big deal. I have all day to clean up. You ladies get ready for church. I can take care of the cleanup." Jalissa wanted to smack the shit out of Krystal for being so damn lazy.

"No, Jalissa, this is what's going happen. You guys cleaned up last night, so we'll do the cleaning this morning. Krystal, you need to stop causing problems this early in the morning and start scraping the dishes. Kristie, you can tidy up the dining room and get off your feet while Krystal and I clean the kitchen," Dior laid down the law.

"Thank you, ladies. I'll be right back after I walk Fallon and Kim to their cars." When they got outside, Jalissa and her home-girls laughed about what just happened in the house.

Krystal moisturized her hands all the way home. She was still a little peeved at Dior for forcing her to clean that ghetto woman's kitchen. She wasn't into manual labor that might injure any part of her body. They could've easily put the dishes in the dishwasher, but no, Dior wanted to wash them by hand. On the drive back to the house, she didn't have much to say to Dior or Kristina. She was glad her sisters were going to church. She did not want to be bothered with either of them right now. When Krystal arrived home from Jalissa's, she made a dash to her room to call Cy.

"Cy, are you going to talk to those agents and get me a better contract?" Krystal didn't even bother saying good morning to Cy.

"Good morning to you, Cy, wouldn't hurt you my, shining star."

"It would be a good morning if you did your job. They are tripping, and you know it."

"Shining star, we've already talked about this, and nothing has changed since the last time we talked. We accepted their offer so just do what you do best, and you'll be at the top before you can blink your beautiful eyes."

"Don't bullshit me, Cy. I'm not having a good morning."

"Okay, I tell you what, give me three months, and if they don't have anything concrete to offer, we can look elsewhere. It would give you major bonus points if you could get Dillon on board."

Krystal went ballistic. "I knew it. All of you are just using me to get to Dillon. How many times and in how many ways does he have to tell you all HE IS OUT of the business?"

"Calm down, shining star. There's no need for you to get upset. And we're not using you to get to Dillon," Cy explained.

"I'm getting off this phone right now before I lose my cool. I need some rest. I'll call you next week." Krystal hung up before Cy could say anything more.

Kristina was exhausted. As soon as she walked in the door from church, she told Reggie she was going to take a nap. Dior brought her suitcase in and told her she would call her later. Reggie followed Kristina up the stairs and handed her a gown to slip into. She was so tired she didn't want to take the time to change, but she knew how uncomfortable she would be trying to sleep in her church clothes.

Once Kristina was asleep, Reggie went back downstairs to finish talking to his mom on the phone. His parents were worried about his little sister, Ashley because she had become quiet and withdrawn. When he went over to talk to Ashley last night she said she was fine, but was a little worried about her classes. Reggie told his mom it was just a teenager thing and he would spend more time with her since he would be off work for a little while. After hanging up the phone, Reggie went into the kitchen to get dinner started. He had seasoned the chicken earlier, so he put it into the oven and assembled the mixed vegetables he wanted to steam. As he was about to see what they would have for dessert, the doorbell rang. Reggie was surprised to see his little sister at the door.

"Ash, what are you doing here? I just got off the phone with mom. She said you were resting in your room."

Ashley grabbed her brother and began to cry. "Reg, can I please come live with you and Kristie?"

"Why do you want to do that?" Reggie escorted his sister into the den and sat down next to her on the loveseat.

"I can't take it over there any longer. If you make me go back, I'll just die." Reggie wished Kristina was up to help him with this situation.

"Baby girl, take a deep breath and tell me what's going on." Reggie knew he should call his mom and let her know Ashley was there, but he had to calm her down first.

"I just can't do this anymore. I have tried so hard, but most of the time, I just want to die so I can have some peace.

"Peace from what? You're really scaring me. What's bothering you, baby girl?"

"It started months ago, but now it's to the point where if I have to go back to that house again, I'll kill myself." Ashley started sobbing again.

"What started months ago?" Reggie was confused.

"Uncle Henry has been messing with me."

"Messing with you how, Ash?"

"Well, last year he started making lewd comments, and then he started touching me."

"Touching you how?"

"On my breast and butt at first and then he started touching other places."

"Ash, why didn't you tell someone?"

"He said if I told, he would tell Mom and Dad that I started it. He said they wouldn't believe me because of all the times I lied to them before."

"Why didn't you tell me? You know I would have been there for you."

"He said it would tear the whole family apart." Ashley began to sob again.

Reggie was so mad it took everything that was within him not to explode. For the second time, he wished Kristina was up to help him with this situation.

Everything is going to be alright baby girl," Reggie said.

"No, it's not. The other night when Mom and Dad were gone he came in my room and tried to rape me."

"Don't worry. You won't have to go back over there. Go upstairs and rest for a while, I will call Mom and let her know you will be staying over here for a while."

Chapter Twenty-Three

Diamond awoke just in time to make it to the bathroom. She started throwing up last night and since then had made three trips to the bathroom. Dillon wanted her to go to the ER, but she explained this was a normal part of pregnancy and refused. She was so sick last night, she didn't even get mad at Dillon and Junior for excluding her from the meetings with the detectives, the clerk from the other hotel, and the firm's investigative team.

The guys didn't find out any new information from the detectives, but they did have productive meetings with the clerk and the firm's investigative team. The clerk told them she found out there were nine couples missing and the last tour they all went on was the Private Las Vegas Mob Tour by Limousine, adding that years ago something similar had happened, but it was put down as friends-playing practical jokes on each other. She told them she had heard some research was being conducted for a study to prove that no matter what walk of life you came from, it could be proven that people are people and the way they react in certain situations was similar.

Dillon and Junior returned to the hotel, and Dillon excused himself to check on Diamond. He found her on the bathroom floor by the stool.

"Baby, I think we should go to the ER, he said, handing her a cool cloth for her face.

"No, this is normal." Diamond reassured him. "How is the case going?"

Dillon filled Diamond in on what he and Junior discovered from their meetings, and she was excited and disappointed by how much they had accomplished.

Nick was relieved to reunite with Bethany. All they could do was hug one another.

The hosts from the men and women's group filtered into the room.

"Ladies and gentlemen, may we please have your attention." The host had to repeat this three times before the room quieted.

"We want all of you to know we are set to depart in thirty minutes to take you back to your respective hotels."

"Why the hell have we been detained against our wills and separated from our wives?" An angry gentleman with a British accent cut off the host

"I know this ordeal may have been an inconvenience, but believe us when we say this study was conducted with all of your mutual consent."

"Bullshit, we didn't sign up for any crazy shit like this." An African-American/Asian man of mixed ethnicity yelled out. "All of this will be explained by your hotel's management staff when you get back." The host insisted.

"We want answers now," demanded the guy with the British accent.

"We WILL NOT answer any additional questions. All of you will be able to get your answers from your hotel management staff." The female host nodded to her co-speaker and they left the room without another word to the confused couples.

Diamond was tossing and turning, but Dillon didn't want to wake her up. Junior was in his room and they all were supposed to meet later for lunch. Diamond sat up suddenly and rushed to the bathroom, startling Dillon. He wanted to follow behind her, but knew she wanted some privacy. Dillon wanted this baby badly, but he hoped like hell Diamond wouldn't have to suffer much longer like this. Thankfully, she looked much better when she came out of the bathroom.

Diamond had a big smile on her face and said with certainty.

"My parents are okay, and I know we're going to find them soon.

"Wow…Okay. Baby, where is this coming from?"

"I had a dream, Dillon, and it was too real for it not to be true. I dreamed my parents were safe, and we all went home and had a big celebration at my parents' house."

"That's really hopeful, baby."

"I can't wait to tell them about the baby. Will it be okay to tell them when they are found instead of waiting until we get back home?" Diamond asked.

"Sure, baby. We can do it however you want. You're right about telling the others when we get home. I can't wait to see the look on my parents' faces.

"Thank you for being so understanding." Diamond's cell phone rang.

"Hey, big bro. what's up?"

"You guys need to get to the lobby right away." Junior didn't say anything else before he hung up.

Diamond relayed Junior's strange call to Dillon, and he rushed to get ready. By the time Diamond and Dillon made it downstairs, there was a big crowd in the lobby. Dillon was pissed at Junior for calling his wife down with all the commotion, but then he caught a glimpse of his father-in-law. He gently took Diamond's hand and escorted her to a quiet corner.

"Di, I just caught a glimpse of your dad."

"Where?" Diamond asked looking around.

"He's clustered in the crowd. I need you to stay here while I go see what's going on."

"Baby, you know that's not going to happen. If my parents are here, there's nothing or no one that will keep me from getting to them."

"Di, please. I need you to listen to me. We don't know what's going on or if this crowd will get rowdy. I promise to come back as soon as I find out what's going on," Dillon pleaded.

"Okay." Diamond nodded. "But make sure you don't take too long."

Dillon made his way through the crowd and, spotted Junior with two of the people from the investigative team. Once he had Junior's attention, they all met on the other side of the lobby.

"Man, this is the greatest day. I saw Dad and Mama Beth, but I couldn't get close enough to talk to them. The word is they have to meet with the hotel's management and the police before they can return to their rooms."

"God is so good. Let's go give Di the good news."

Chapter Twenty-Four

Kristina was still trying to cope with Ashley's devastating news. The tears in her husband's eyes were heartbreaking. For a moment, Kristina thought perhaps he had heard bad news about her parents, and her heart sank to the bottom of her stomach. Then, he told her about Ashley and she could not believe her ears. He asked if it was okay for Ashley to stay with them until things were sorted out. Kristina agreed and held her husband. Kristina's cell phone rang, interrupting her thoughts about her sister-in-law. She answered, happy to hear Junior's voice.

"How's it going, big brother?"

"Are you sitting down, Kristie?"

"Oh my God, please don't have bad news about Mom and Dad."

"No, sweetie. It's great news. Dad and Mama Beth are back at the hotel. We haven't had a chance to talk to them though."

"Are you serious, Junior?"

"Yes, I wouldn't joke about this. Could you do me a big favor? Call the rest of the family? You are the first person I called. I want to call Jalissa, and that may take a while."

"Thanks, Junior. I'll spread the word."

"Our prayers have been answered."

"Indeed, they have, big brother. I'll talk to you later." Kristina ended her call and yelled for Reggie. He was upstairs in five seconds flat.

"Is it the baby? Are you alright?"

"They found my parents, and they're okay." Kristina said, with tears in her eyes.

"That's great news. Do you need me to make any calls?"

"If you call both sets of grandparents, I'll call Krystal and the others."

Dior arrived home a little later than usual and was surprised to see all the lights on in the house. She found Krystal dancing in the living room with the music blasting. Dior yelled her name three times and finally turned the stereo off. When Krystal saw Dior standing in the doorway, she ran to her sister and gave her a big hug.

"What's up, baby girl?"

"We didn't want to bother you at work, but they found Mom and Dad, and they're okay."

"Thank you, Jesus."

The doorbell rang before Dior could say anymore. She opened the door to a host of family who walked in and headed toward the dining room. Happy tears shone in all of their faces.

"I knew she would do it. I knew Di would find my baby," Bethany's mom said.

"Grandma Stacey, we don't know all the details yet. We don't know what role, if any, Di played in finding Mom and Dad." Krystal rolled her eyes.

"I know she had something to do with it. And even if she didn't, at least she took the time to go and see about her parents."

"Where's the rest of the family?" Dior asked wanting to change the subject.

"Kristie stayed home so she could rest up for your parents return tomorrow, and Vince and Stan will be here within the hour," Grandma Eunice said.

Dior glanced at her Auntie Denise and wondered why she was so quiet. She seemed to be in her own little world.

"Well, I can't wait to talk to that boy and hear what really happened. He better have a good excuse for worrying his poor mama. Maybe we could look at some family videos until we get a call from Vegas. All this small talk isn't keeping our minds off what's going on." Nick's dad, Justin said.

"That's a good idea, Grandfather. Why don't all of you go into the den while Krystal and I bring in some refreshments?" Dior suggested.

The conference room was crowded with people for the debriefing. The three couples from Caesars Palace all wore scowls on their faces while the two detectives that had spoken with Diamond tried to comprehend what took place weeks ago, and why none of the three hotels' management staff let them in on what was happening.

"We need to wrap this up so we can reunite with our families. No matter what the hell games you all are playing, this is far from over," Nick said.

"Look, Mr. Morgan, we have promised to reimburse your hotel stay and pick up the tab for any expenses incurred by your family members," Mr. Pittman said. "I know you're anxious to see your family, but really, I don't see what the big deal is. The hotels are the ones who will lose a small fortune from this experiment gone wrong."

"You, pompous ass! There's no price tag you can place on our family's emotions. We have a high-risk pregnant daughter that didn't need this added stress." Nick growled at the hotel manager.

"Sir, I apologized. I don't mean to appear insensitive. But, we have said and done all we can in regards to this situation. Unless the detectives have anything else to add, you all are free to go," Mr. Pittman said.

"We don't have anything further at the moment, but if all of you would be kind enough to leave your contact information, that would be helpful for us," Detective Plummer said.

Nick looked at the detective like he was crazy. "All I want to do is leave the hell out of Vegas. Too bad the earliest flight out isn't until tomorrow afternoon."

Junior dreaded the next call he had to make, but he wanted to hurry and finish his calls so he could go and meet with the others in his dad's suite. He dialed his mom's number. Hearing her in a happy mood almost made him hang up, since he knew his news would spoil her good mood.

"Hi, Ma. How have you been doing?"

"About time you took a minute out of your busy schedule to call your mom. What did I do to deserve your ignoring me?"

"I'm not ignoring you, Ma. I've talked to you twice since I've been here." Junior rolled his eyes.

"And how many times have you talked to that wife of yours or those other creatures?"

"Ma, please don't start. I only have a few minutes. I just wanted to see how you were doing and let you know how things are going here."

"I don't want to know how things are going there. All I want to know is when are you coming home?"

"I'll be home tomorrow evening, and I'll come by for a visit sometime the day after. I know you don't care, but Dad and Beth are back at the hotel, and they're doing fine." Junior held his breath for his mom's smart remark.

"You damn skippy I don't care. So why bother telling me?"

"Good God, Ma. Can't you just think back to a time when you use to love Dad and be happy that he's alive and well for my sake and the sake of your grandson?"

"Boy, let me get off this phone right now before you make me lose my religion. Why the hell should I feel anything for that man but pure hatred?"

"You should care because if you keep going on like this, you're going to end up alone and bitter with no one to blame but yourself."

"So what are you saying? You're going to walk out on me too like all the other idiots that claim to care about me?"

"No, Ma, I won't walk out on you. But you are making it very difficult to stay around you with all the hate you keep spreading."

"Just make the arrangements for my damn trip and maybe I won't come back. Then you won't have to worry about being around a person you consider to be so hateful."

Chapter Twenty-Five

Nick and Bethany went to their room, but Diamond grabbed both of them into a big hug before they could enter.

"It's good to see you both alive and well." Dillon said a little teary eyed.

"Thanks, Dillon" Nick and Bethany said at the same time.

"Well, it's so damn good to see all of you. How are you doing, son?" Nick asked Junior.

"I'm doing great, sir, now that I know both of you are safe." Junior went over, hugged Bethany and shook his dad's hand. But his dad surprised him and pulled him into an embrace.

"I know you guys want to get some rest, but if we can make a call home, it would put the family's mind at ease. Everyone is at your house except for Kristie," Diamond said.

"We are exhausted, but I won't rest, until I've checked on everyone at home. I know you guys must have been worried sick about us," Bethany said through tears.

Diamond nodded. "We were, and I know everyone will want to speak to you so maybe we should call Kristie first."

"Okay, but first, how are you doing, Di? You look a little worn out," Bethany asked.

"I'm good, Mom," Diamond said.

Junior went to the other side of the room and dialed Kristie's number from the hotel's phone. He spoke with Reggie for a minute and then handed the phone to Bethany.

"Kristie, stop crying. We are both safe and sound. You know your dad is too stubborn to stay away too long." Bethany assured her daughter.

"Mom, I'm so relieved both of you are okay. I prayed God would answer my prayers, and He did in a big way."

"Me too, Baby. Now let's plan talk more tomorrow. We have to call the rest of the family and let them know we're okay. But, I'll let you talk to your dad for a few minutes. I love you, baby cakes." Bethany handed Nick the phone. After talking to Kristina for a few minutes, he called home to speak to the rest of the family.

Kristina was happy to talk to her parents, but she felt bad for her husband. He had to tell the parents he loved and adored that they couldn't come over because Ashley wasn't ready to see them. They didn't understand what was going on and wanted to get to the bottom of the problem, but backed off when Reggie told them how fragile Ashley was emotionally. They were devastated that Ashley felt suicidal, but at this point, Reggie felt he had to be more concerned about his sister's feelings than his parents. Ashley had told him she tried on two different occasions to bring the issue up with their mom, but she did not want to hear or talk about it. He knew he could not send his sister back home. Still, Reggie could not believe all of this was going on under his parents' roof without their knowledge.

Reggie was able to talk Ashley into seeing their parents tomorrow.

"Baby, I want to spend the night at my parents' house tomorrow, but I feel like I'm abandoning you to deal with this situation alone," Kristina said.

No, Kristie, I don't want you home when my parents come over tomorrow. I don't know how ugly this is going to get. Plus, you need to be with your parents and the rest of the family on their first day back."

"Are you going to keep calm and hear your parents out? All of this could have happened without their knowing."

"Of course, I'll hear them out. I just don't like to see my baby sister going through all this pain, especially when it could've been avoided. My dad has to realize he can't be responsible for a grown ass man like his brother if he continues to cause trouble like he has most of his adult life."

"Baby, calm down. You can find the underlying cause tomorrow. Give me a chance to talk to Ashley. Maybe she'll be more open talking to a female."

"Kristie, I really don't want you stressed out by this situation."

"I want to help. When we are done with dinner tonight, I'll have a long talk with Ashley. If she doesn't feel like talking, I won't push her."

"Okay, baby, we'll leave it at that, and hope and pray for the best. I just want to put the smile back on my sister's face."

Nick knew he should be happy the hotel was reimbursing them for the entire trip, but he felt like a fool for not being more careful about what he was signing. His friend Vince had laughed at him which pissed Nick off even more. He knew the best things in life weren't free, and his inner critic had "dumbass" on constant repeat. Nick was ashamed that he allowed himself to be gullible. How could an attorney be swindled?

"Okay, kids. I know you all are anxious to find out what happened. Let me give you the short version because we all need to rest. To give credit where it's due, if I had listened to my dear wife, we wouldn't have been in this position."

"Honey, I told you to stop blaming yourself. You just wanted us to experience something different and exciting."

"Thanks, babe, but this is definitely my fault, and I'll take full responsibility. Our trip was going well. We had seen several shows, been on a few tours, even took the time to play tables and slots. It was my bright idea to go on the tour from hell. The advertisement was so exciting I wanted to give it a try. It started off with the highlights of the tour which were the private limousine ride. The men were dressed in pinstriped suits telling stories about some of the rumors behind this city's mysterious mob connections."

"Honey, you're taking the long way around something that could be explained in a few sentences. We unknowingly signed a document stating we would be part of a study that was being conducted by some researchers in town. This research consisted of assembling a group of people together from different cultural and economic backgrounds to see how they would react in an uncontrolled environment. The husbands and wives had to be separated for a certain period of time to survey and record their reactions to different situations..."

Diamond was laughing so hard tears were running down her face.

"Okay oldest daughter of mine. What the hell is so funny?" Nick asked.

"I'm sorry, Dad, but I know you and the other two attorneys didn't get sucked into signing a ridiculous agreement without your knowledge. Law 101 tells you to always read the fine print."

"We're not going to talk about the law right now. As a matter of fact, we can finish this conversation tomorrow so all of us can get some overdue rest." Nick stood and opened the door to their suite.

Junior chuckled, "See Di, you had to ruin everything. Now we're going to have to wait until tomorrow to hear the rest of this adventure."

"Come on, big brother, you know good and well Dad wasn't going to tell us the entire story."

"Let me get you back to our room, Di, before I have to see you get a spanking." Dillon laughed. "The look on your dad's face is telling you to cut it out."

"We'll see you guys in the morning for breakfast." Nick said, as the kids left.

Chapter Twenty-Six

Diamond and Dillon sat together on one side of the plane headed home. Her parents were on the other side and Junior was farther back with the investigative team. They had agreed at breakfast not to discuss her parents' ordeal again until they got home. There was a relieved look on her dad's face. Since they weren't going to talk about the ordeal, Diamond decided it was time to tell them about the baby. She had taken a sip of tea and cleared her throat to get her parents' full attention.

"Mom, Dad, I have some news to share with you guys. I'm pregnant."

"Thank you, Jesus," Bethany said, standing to hug Diamond and Dillon.

"What's wrong, Dad?" Diamond had asked.

"Nothing, it's just…I thought you were going to wait a while to start a family?" Nick said.

"Well, I thought so too, but I didn't want to wait too long. Besides, I think it's great that our baby will be close in age to Kristie's."

"I guess you're right about that. I think we made a mistake having two sets of children so far apart. That may have played a role in why you and Krystal are always at each other's throat."

"No, the problem is we all spoiled that girl rotten and now no one can stand to be around her."

"Well, I hope all of that will change now. We have to come together as a family and stop dealing with our lives as individual parts." Bethany threw her napkin on the table.

"Dad, are you happy about our good news?" Diamond didn't like the blank look on her dad's face.

"Of course, I am. It's just... I was going to take a step back for a while to figure out what to do about our Vegas ordeal."

"You can still do that, Dad. I can handle the firm for a while."

"Not for long," Nick and Dillon said in unison, drawing laughter from everyone at the table.

"Wait a minute, I love both of you very much, but don't expect me to put my career on hold because I'm having a baby," Diamond said.

"Now, on hold, baby. We just want you to take it easy." Dillon said.

"Both of you cut it out. Women have been having babies and working for centuries without living like an invalid. Stop ganging up on Di," Bethany said.

"It's okay, Mom. I got this." Diamond looked at her dad and her husband. "I appreciate the concern from both of you, but I'll be fine handling the business if you want to take some time off, Dad."

Nick and Bethany's house was full of people to welcome the Vegas group back home.

Even Jalissa was there, though it had taken Dior and Kristina close to a half hour to persuade her to join them. The duo told Jalissa if this situation has taught them anything it was about how precious life was and how they needed to work together as a family.

Bethany entered her home and went straight to her mom and mother-in-law. The other women circled the crying ladies. The guys chatted in the background until Nick and the rest of the Vegas group excused themselves to freshen up for dinner. The catered food had the house smelling of soul food, and there was excitement around the table. Everyone was relieved to have Nick and Bethany home. After dinner and dessert, the ladies cleaned and the men went into the family room.

Nick didn't want to tell everyone what really happened to them, but knew there was no way around it. Bethany tried to help, but made things worse when she told everyone not to give her husband a hard time.

"I'll make this long story short and simple. Beth and I signed up to go on the Private Mob Tour. It started off like it was supposed to with our being picked up in a limousine by tour guides in pinstriped suits along with two other couples from the hotel. They told us stories of Las Vegas' mysterious past.

"To back up a little bit, when I signed us up for the tour, I failed to check the fine print and the addendum which just tickled my darling oldest daughter's funny bone. Anyway, when we got to the place where they said Tupac Shakur was gunned down, everything went black. My next conscious moment was being in a room with eight other men, but I only recognized the two from our hotel."

"Son, do you remember getting on Di when she first started out about reading every single word in a document no matter who gave it to her before signing it?" Nick's dad asked with a smile on his face. "I guess it was right funny to her that her sophisticated dad didn't heed his own words."

"Come on, Pop. Don't rub salt into an open wound." Nick said, continuing his story when everyone stopped laughing.

"I don't think they were able to collect the data they needed because most of us refused to play their games, participate in discussions, or consent to individual hypnosis which is how they got us all in one place.

"So, you guys were hypnotized during the tour and that's how they got all of you in one place at the same time?" Vince smirked.

"Do you all want me to continue or not?" Nick asked.

"Baby, go on and finish your story. You all need to leave Nicky alone and stop making fun of my son," Eunice said.

"Thanks, Mom." Nick rubbed his mother's knee in appreciation of her defense. "Anyway, we all need to get settled in, so let me finish. They wanted to conduct a study of how people would react to being in an environment where they were forced to stay. The group was diverse, and they needed to observe the women and men separately to get accurate results.

"I think we've heard enough for tonight." Dior interrupted. "Mom, Dad, it's so good to have you back home, but you look exhausted."

"Dior is right. I am ready to get some rest," Bethany said.

Chapter Twenty-Seven

Reggie's parents walked in the door of his home. His mom, Rosa grabbed her daughter and gave her a big hug. Then, their dad did the same. Reggie and Ashley had prepared food for their parents and asked if they were hungry. Their parents declined and Reggie's dad got straight to the point.

"Okay, somebody better tell me what the hell is going on. First, your mama tells me Ashley will be staying with you and Kristie for a little while and then when we get up this morning, there's no sight of Henry."

"Dad, I need you not to mention that man's name in my home again please," Reggie said politely.

"What's going on, Son? I'm confused by this entire situation. Ash, what's wrong with you?" Their dad asked.

"I'll tell you what's going on, Dad. That good for nothing brother of yours been molesting, Ash for months."

The shocked looks on their parents' faces confirmed to Reggie his parents had no idea what was going on in their household. Tears ran down their mom's face, and Ashley started to sob.

Reggie could tell his dad was mad by his clinched fists.

"Ash, why didn't you tell somebody what was going on? I'm going to kill that rotten bastard." Their dad, Howard paced back and forth.

"How could he do something so horrible to my baby? That explains why he disappeared, but he can't hide forever."

"You need to calm down, honey. We need to see to Ashley's needs, not worry about finding that low-down fool." Reggie's mother said.

"Mama, I tried to tell you more than once, but you wouldn't listen to me," Ashley said.

"I'm so sorry, baby. My mind has been somewhere else. I should have listened to you." She glanced at her husband.

"What your mama isn't telling you is that I have prostate cancer, and she's been so busy worrying about me, she didn't see what was going on with our baby. This situation is so messed up. I feel like the worse father in the world." Their dad's explanation shocked them both.

"How could you guys keep this from us? We had a right to know," Reggie said.

"Baby, I'm sorry. It was my idea not to tell you kids. We found out six weeks ago." Rosa wrung her hands. "I didn't want y'all to worry about something you can't do anything about."

"But we're a family, Ma. And families stick together," Reggie said before they prayed and ate their meal.

Diamond intended to work on Phil's case, but her stomach had other ideas. When she came out of the bathroom, Dillon was sitting up in bed with a sad look on his face. "Baby, I don't know if I can stand seeing you this sick."

"This isn't going to last forever. Just think about our bundle of joy. He or she is well worth what I'm going through right now."

"When are you going to make your doctor's appointment? I'll feel much better knowing all is well with you and the baby."

"I'll call later today. I want to do some work on Phil's case before I go over to my parents. Are you going to the center today?"

"Yes, but just to check in and see how things are going. Do you think you can go over to my parents' house with me around noon? I want you to be with me when I tell them about the baby."

"Sure, I'll work a couple hours on Phil's case, make my doctor's appointment, and then get ready. I can go over to my parents afterwards. Do you want to be there when I tell the rest of the family today?"

"I do. I can make it over there around four o'clock."

"Good, we can tell them after dinner. I know all the grandparents will be there, and Dior said she would stop by after work."

"What about Kristie? I know you've been anxious to tell her."

"She's still over there. Reggie is picking her up later tonight."

"Okay, baby, let me shower so I can get my day started. I'll see you at my parents' around noon."

"I can't believe it's taken more than a dozen years, but yesterday was the first time I actually felt like a part of your family," Jalissa said.

"I told you things were going to change after this incident." Junior had a big smile on his face.

"Well, I hope this means better times for Joe."

"It will and speaking of Joe, have you given my earlier suggestion any thought?"

"What suggestion, honey bunch?" When Junior told her about Diamond being pregnant, she knew she wasn't going to escape this topic for long.

"The one where I asked you about us having another baby, I know you didn't forget."

"Junior, why do you keep bringing this up? How many times have I told you Joe was it?"

"I know, baby, but with Kristie and Di having babies this year, I thought it would be nice to make it a threesome."

"Oh my God, Junior, when are you going to stop competing with Di? You will NEVER take her place in your dad's heart or business."

"I'm not competing with Di. I don't want to be a Nick Jr., even though I have his name. Di can have that title all by herself."

"Instead of trying to procreate, why don't you try to make inroads with your dad?"

"We're fine, baby. I think he even missed me. He said we'll talk privately soon."

"There you go again, grasping at the crumbs he's throwing your way."

"Let's change the subject. Are you going over to Dad and Mama Beth's with me later?"

"No, I don't want to push my luck. Plus, I'm going over to visit Joe after work."

"Okay, tell him I'll see him tomorrow at his after-school program."

"Make sure you don't forget or make other plans. He's counting on you."

"I got this." Junior kissed Jalissa. "I have a few errands to run before I go to the big house. I'll see you later."

Chapter Twenty-Eight

Junior didn't want to tell Jalissa one of the errands he had to run was to visit his mom. He pulled in his mom's driveway and mentally prepared himself for a lecture he knew he was going to hear. He was taken by surprise when the door opened before he had a chance to ring the bell.

"Baby, it's so good to see you. Come on in," Him mom said.

"Hey, Ma, how are you doing today?" Junior wondered what was going on with his mom. She seemed to be in a good mood a lot lately.

"I'm feeling great. I just got back from shopping for my trip."

"Good, that's what I came to talk to you about. You're scheduled to leave on Sunday, the seventeenth and return on Sunday, the twenty-fourth."

"That's great, baby. I'm so excited. I've been doing some research. I know exactly how I want to spend my time."

"I'm proud of you, Ma. I'll get with the rest of the family to start collecting your spending money. I'll be back over in a few days to bring your itinerary." Junior wondered why his mom didn't have anything to say. Ma, I was thinking, maybe we should get together before you leave and have a small dinner party. Something nice. We can have it at my house or at a restaurant."

"I'm so happy I won't even let that bring me down. You can plan a small dinner at your house on Sunday, the tenth. Do I get to say who can come?"

"Yes, Ma, to lessen the stress, it will be just the four of us, and I can give you the money that's collected at that time. It would be nice to thank everyone before you leave."

"You're asking too much. I have my own spending money. If I have to thank them, then, I don't want the money," Melissa said.

"Ma, please stop this foolishness. We've been blessed. We need to share the blessings."

"You're asking me to overcome too much at one time. I'm working on it, so you're going to have to be satisfied with that for now."

"Okay, Ma, have it your way. I'll be in touch soon with the details for our dinner. I have to go now. I have a few more errands to run." Junior gave his mom a hug and left so he could finish what he had to do before going over to his dad's.

All the Morgan family and close friends met for dinner at Nick and Bethany's. Krystal wanted to stay upstairs, but Nick made her come down and eat with the rest of the family. Nick's dad, Justin blessed the food. Halfway through the meal, Bethany couldn't hold it in any longer.

"Di is pregnant," She squealed.

The whole room quieted.

"This is the greatest news." Kristina clapped. "Our babies are going to have a ball together."

"Congratulations, Di. I know you're going to make an excellent mom," Denise said.

"Oh my God, you guys need to chill. You all acting like she just won a gold medal. It's just a baby," Krystal said.

"You need to shut your mouth if you don't have anything nice to say to my wife, Krystal," Dillon said.

"Baby, it's okay. You know Krystal can't stand it when the world isn't revolving around her, but even she can't ruin this joyous moment." Diamond grabbed Dillon's hand.

"Krystal, come with me right now," Bethany demanded.

"Di, we're so happy for you. Just think, we're going to have two great-grandchildren to spoil this Christmas." Eunice lifted her hands heavenward. "Dear Lord, thank you for two healthy babies. Amen."

"Thanks, Grandmother." Everyone laughed when both Diamond and Kristina said the same thing at the same time.

Bethany and Krystal came back into the room with a different look on their faces than when they left. Krystal apologized to Diamond and everyone else at the table, and the night was filled with so much joy and love.

Three Months Later

At four and a half months, Diamond and Dillon were shocked to learn they were expecting twins. It would be another month or so, depending on the cooperation of the babies, before they knew the sex. Diamond hoped her initial wish would come true and they would have a boy and girl.

Now, Diamond sat in her office, thinking about the good luck she had with Phil's case.

Dillon didn't like her spending so much time on it, but since she was done with her morning sickness, he was a little less stressed.

Phil's case was settled with a plea bargain, and he didn't have to spend any time in jail. He was ordered to do two hundred hours of community service, take anger management counseling, and was placed on two years' probation. He made arrangements with Dillon to do his community service at the youth center. Dillon made it clear Phil would have to work as hard as others around the center.

Diamond was so glad for her sister's health that Ashley was able to go home and mend her relationship with her parents. She was proud of how well Kristina and Reggie handled the situation. She prayed the last few months of Kristina's pregnancy would go as scheduled.

They hadn't heard from Henry since he packed up and left the Burns household. Reggie and Ashley's father wanted to hunt him down, but his health issues wouldn't allow him. He was now at stage four cancer and had stopped taking treatments since they weren't working. Although they were hoping he would be around for the baby's birth, they all knew his chances were slim. Kristina and Reggie had decided to name their daughter Miracle Holly. The first name was for their daughter possibly saving her dad's life when he had raced home to check on Kristina and avoided the bank robbery. Her middle name was for Reggie's dad, Howard Lee.

Diamond was glad her dad was able to let the Vegas case go after a while. Turned out Junior's instincts about the clerk at the other hotel were right. She was part of the group that screened the couples for the experiment. She made sure only the right candidates went on that particular tour and was the point person for all three hotels. Because all couples had signed the agreement and addendum, they didn't have any legal grounds to pursue a lawsuit, so Nick had to be satisfied with the financial reimbursement the hotel had given them.

Junior knocked on Diamond's door.

Diamond looked up at her big brother and smiled. She felt sorry for him. Jalissa had her tubes tied so he wouldn't keep hoping she would change her mind about having another baby. Junior was sad for a long time until Diamond scheduled a meeting with their dad to discuss Junior's professional future at the firm. After working for two months and getting familiar with the firm's business practices, Nick promoted Junior to Head of Security. He also gave Junior access to his trust fund, but not before Melissa's trip. Nick stressed the money was for Junior and his immediate family, Jalissa and Joe.

"Hey, sis, got a few minutes?"

"Come on in, big brother. I was just about to pack up and go home for the day."

"Well, I'm glad I caught you. I was wondering if you, Dad and I could get together sometime this week."

"It's fine with me. We just need to check with Dad. You want to tell me what this is about?"

"It's about the business plan for Dior's daycare. I was thinking about seeing if she would go for Jalissa being her partner. Jalissa is looking for a change, and since she was an accounting major at the university, she could be of help in that area. I figured if all three of us approached, Dior with a proposal, she might go for it."

"Dior is level headed. Why couldn't you have a meeting with her yourself? Have you brought this subject up to Jalissa?"

"No, not directly. But, I know she wants a change. Plus, if we do it this way, we can keep the business in the family, and Dior wouldn't have to seek outside financing."

"Maybe, we shouldn't bother Dad with this. I can draw up the necessary paperwork and handle any other legal issues."

"Okay, I can talk to Jalissa tonight when I get home. Are you available this Saturday for dinner? I can talk to Dior and see if she'll be free."

"As far as I know, we don't have anything planned. I just need to check with Dillon. I still can't get over all the money and free publicity he's getting for the center since he went back to modeling."

"When you got it, you got it. Even though I miss her evil ass, Krystal is really doing well in New York."

"I'm just glad they came through for her. I got tired of hearing her complaining about how they used her to get to Dillon."

"It's sad, Di, but it's true. They did use our baby sister to get to your husband. But that's the way business works in that industry, so she better get used to it."

"I have to get out of here, big bro. I'll give you a call about Saturday after I talk to Dillon."

"Okay, sis, see you later."

Diamond packed up her belongings and left about five minutes after Junior.

Epilogue

Dillon couldn't feel his right hand after the tight squeeze Diamond gave from that last contraction. He hoped the babies would be born soon. If not, Diamond would have to have a C-section. She was able to carry almost to full-term. They were the happiest couple alive when they found out they were having a set of boy and girl twins. Two months ago, when Miracle Holly Burns was born, the parents, grandparents, and great-grand parents had this same hospital on emotional lockdown. The seven-pound, eight-ounce, beauty made her entrance into the world on July 25th at 4:40 p.m. after Kristina had a long, hard eight-hour labor.

Krystal shocked everyone when she came home for the delivery. It was the first time she'd been back since she left to begin her modeling career with Kendra and Brian. The only thing that took the joy of Miracle's birth away was the fact that Howard lost his battle with prostate cancer six weeks before Miracle's birth. He died in the comfort of his home with his wife and daughter by his side. Kristina felt saddened because Reggie, his mom, and his baby sister had suffered for a long time.

The doctor told Diamond the first baby's head was crowning, and she just needed to give one more big push. Diamond pushed, almost crushing Dillon's hand in the process. She could hear the baby crying. She wanted to hold her baby, but knew she was only half done.

"Baby, it's Kyle. He's here." Dillon was ecstatic, but Diamond started to cry and told Dillon to go get her mom and Kristina.

"I'll get your mom, but it wouldn't be fair to get Kristie when your other sisters are out there too." Krystal was home for two weeks to do a photo shoot with Dillon. Her attitude had been much better since that time at dinner when their mom had a talk with her.

"Whatever, you never listen to me." Dillon knew Diamond didn't mean what she said. It was the drugs talking. Bethany made it into the room, and two minutes later, Kayla Lynette Washington was born. Four minutes after her big brother Kyle Austin Washington. Kyle was the bigger of the twins weighing in at six pounds, four ounces, and twenty-one inches while Kayla was five pounds, two ounces, and twenty inches. Bethany went to the waiting room to tell the rest of the family about the babies, marveling that for the first time in their lives, the family seemed to pull together.

Melissa was finally being a grandma to Joe, and now they were inseparable. They didn't know what happened to Melissa on her birthday trip, but whatever it was, she came back more relaxed and approachable. She was even getting along a little better with Jalissa. Junior was content because he didn't have to walk on eggshells any longer when he brought up his dad and other family members. All of Melissa's nasty comments stopped.

With the major changes in Krystal and Melissa, the Morgan family felt secure in knowing that all things are possible if you have faith in the Lord. As Diamond gazed down into the faces of her twins, she realized she could have it all. She'd won the battle of a lifetime when she was able to plea out Phil's case. She smiled, exhausted, happy and content. Fighting for truth, justice, and the American way really can serve its purpose.

Discussion Questions

Listed below are potential questions that can be used for a book club discussion:

Story/Characters

1) What scene in the book was the most important? What difference would it had made if the scene wasn't in the book?

2) Do you think Diamond was too bossy towards her sisters?

3) Were there any surprises in the book that was compelling? If yes, what were they?

4) Why do you think Diamond and Krystal don't get along?

5) Why do you think Junior didn't have any bad feelings towards his sisters?

6) Were you able to guess what would happen in any of the storylines?

7) Why do you think the men were so easily tricked into signing the permission forms?

8) Do you think the agents from New York and Cy used Krystal to get to Dillon?

9) Was it hard to relate to any of the characters in the book?

10) Do you think it was unfair of Jalissa not to consider having another child since Junior wanted another one badly?

11) What do you think happened on Melissa's trip to bring about her drastic change of behavior?

12) Were there any points in the book where you disagreed with one of the character's choices?

<u>Overall</u>

1) Have you read any other books by Diana Carter? If yes, how were they compared to this book?

2) What, if anything did you take away from this book?

3) What would you like to see this author do next?

4) How would you rate the author's overall storytelling abilities?

www.ingramcontent.com/pod-product-compliance
Lightning Source LLC
Chambersburg PA
CBHW021017120726
47905CB00009B/3061